The Voice at J

B. M. Bower

Alpha Editions

This edition published in 2024

ISBN : 9789362994417

Design and Setting By
Alpha Editions
www.alphaedis.com
Email - info@alphaedis.com

As per information held with us this book is in Public Domain.
This book is a reproduction of an important historical work. Alpha Editions uses the best technology to reproduce historical work in the same manner it was first published to preserve its original nature. Any marks or number seen are left intentionally to preserve its true form.

Contents

CHAPTER ONE PATRICIA ENTERTAINS ....- 1 -
CHAPTER TWO PATRICIA EXPLAINS ....- 6 -
CHAPTER THREE PATRICIA TAKES HER STAND..........- 11 -
CHAPTER FOUR GARY GOES ON THE WARPATH..........- 15 -
CHAPTER FIVE GARY DOES A LITTLE SLEUTHING......- 18 -
CHAPTER SIX JOHNNYWATER..- 24 -
CHAPTER SEVEN THE VOICE ....- 28 -
CHAPTER EIGHT "THE CAT'S GOT 'EM TOO!" ....- 31 -
CHAPTER NINE GARY WRITES A LETTER......................- 36 -
CHAPTER TEN GARY HAS SPEECH WITH HUMAN BEINGS ....- 40 -
CHAPTER ELEVEN "HOW WILL YOU TAKE YOUR MILLIONS?"...- 45 -
CHAPTER TWELVE MONTY APPEARS..............................- 49 -
CHAPTER THIRTEEN "I DON'T BELIEVE IN SPOOKS".- 53 -
CHAPTER FOURTEEN PATRICIA REGISTERS FURY .....- 58 -
CHAPTER FIFTEEN "WHAT'S THE MATTER WITH THIS PLACE?" ....- 64 -
CHAPTER SIXTEEN "THERE'S MYSTERY HERE——"..- 72 -
CHAPTER SEVENTEEN JAMES BLAINE HAWKINS FINDS HIS COURAGE—AND LOSES IT................................- 75 -
CHAPTER EIGHTEEN GARY RIDES TO KAWICH............- 81 -
CHAPTER NINETEEN "HAVE YUH-ALL GOT A GUN?".- 85 -
CHAPTER TWENTY "THAT CAT AIN'T HUMAN!"..........- 89 -
CHAPTER TWENTY-ONE GARY FOLLOWS THE PINTO CAT...- 94 -
CHAPTER TWENTY-TWO THE PAT CONNOLLY MINE - 97 -

CHAPTER TWENTY-THREE GARY FINDS THE VOICE—AND SOMETHING ELSE	- 102 -
CHAPTER TWENTY-FOUR "STEVE CARSON—POOR DEVIL!"	- 107 -
CHAPTER TWENTY-FIVE THE VALUE OF A HUNCH	- 110 -
CHAPTER TWENTY-SIX "GARY MARSHALL MYSTERIOUSLY MISSING"	- 114 -
CHAPTER TWENTY-SEVEN "NOBODY KNOWS BUT A PINTO CAT"	- 117 -
CHAPTER TWENTY-EIGHT MONTY MEETS PATRICIA	- 121 -
CHAPTER TWENTY-NINE GARY ROBS THE PINTO CAT OF HER DINNER	- 125 -
CHAPTER THIRTY "SOMEBODY HOLLERED UP ON THE BLUFF"	- 128 -
CHAPTER THIRTY-ONE "GOD WOULDN'T LET ANYTHING HAPPEN TO GARY!"	- 132 -
CHAPTER THIRTY-TWO "IT'S THE VOICE! IT AIN'T HUMAN!"	- 136 -
CHAPTER THIRTY-THREE "HE'S NEARLY STARVED," SAID PATRICIA	- 139 -
CHAPTER THIRTY-FOUR LET'S LEAVE THEM THERE	- 143 -

CHAPTER ONE
PATRICIA ENTERTAINS

The telephone bell was shrilling insistent summons in his apartment when Gary pushed open the hall door thirty feet away. Even though he took long steps, he hoped the nagging jingle would cease before he could reach the 'phone. But the bell kept ringing, being an automatic telephone, dependent upon no perfunctory Central for the persistency of its call. Gary was tired, and from his neck to his waist his skin was painted a coppery bronze which, having been applied at six-thirty that morning, was now itching horribly as the grease paint dried. He did not feel like talking to any one; but he unlocked his door, jerked down the receiver and barked a surly greeting into the mouthpiece of the 'phone. Almost immediately the wrinkles on his forehead slid down into smoothness.

"Oh, *how*-do, Gary! I was just wondering if you had changed your apartments or something," called the girl whom he hoped some day to marry. "Did you just get in?"

"No-o—certainly not! I've been having a fit on the floor! Say, I heard you ringing the 'phone a block away. Every tenant in the joint is lined up on the sidewalk, watching for the Black Maria or the ambulance; they don't know which. But I recognized your ring. What's on your mind, Girlie?"

"Not a thing in the world but a new shell comb. If I'd known you were so terrifically cross this evening, I wouldn't have a lovely dinner all waiting and a great big surprise for you afterwards. Now I won't tell you what it is. And, furthermore, I shall not give you even a hint of what you're going to eat when you get here. But I should think a man who could recognize a certain telephone ring a block away might smell fried chicken and strawberry shortcake clear across the city—with oodles of butter under the strawberries, and double cream———"

"Oh-h, *boy!*" Gary brightened and smacked his lips into the mouthpiece, just as any normal young man would do. Then, recalling his physical discomfort, he hedged a little.

"Will it keep? I'm in a starving condition as usual—but listen, Pat; I'm a savage under my shirt. Just got in from location away up in Topanga Cañon, and I never stopped to get off anything but the rainbow on my cheeks and my feathered war bonnet. Had a heck of a day—I'll tell the world! You know, honey; painted warriors hurtling down the cliff shooting poisoned arrows at the hapless emigrants—*that* kind of hokum. Big Chief Eagle Eye has been hurtling and whooping war whoops since ten o'clock this morning. Dinner'll have to wait while I take a bath and clean up a little. I look like a bum and that's a fact. Say, listen, honey——"

"Aw, take that mush off the line. Ha-ang up!" Some impatient neighboring tenant with a bad temper was evidently cutting in.

"Aw, go lead yourself out by the ear!" Gary retorted sharply. "Say, Pat!" His voice softened to the wooing note of the young male human. "Best I can do, honey, it'll be forty minutes. That's giving me ten minutes to look like a white man again. You know it'll take me thirty minutes to ride out there——"

"You could walk, you bum, whilst you're tellin' her about it. Get off the line! There ought to be a law against billy-cooin' over the 'phone——"

"Seddown! You're rockin' the boat!" Gary flung back spiritedly. "Better make it forty-five, Girlie. It may take me five minutes to lick this cheap heavy on the third floor that's tryin' to put on a comedy act."

"Say, one more crack like that an' I'll be down to your place an' save yuh some valuable time. It'll take me about two seconds to knock yuh cold!" The harsh male voice interrupted eagerly.

"Are you there, Pat?"

"Right here, Gary. How did *that* get into a respectable house, dear? You ought to call the janitor." The girl he hoped to marry had spirit and could assuredly hold her own in a wicked city. "Take your time, Gary boy. But remember, I've the biggest surprise in your life waiting for you out here. Something *wonderful!*"

It is astonishing how a woman can pronounce a few simple words so that they sound like a hallelujah chorus of angels. Gary thrilled to her voice, in spite of an intensely practical nature. Patricia went on, after an impressive pause.

"Never mind that noise in the 'phone, Gary. It's just some mechanical deficiency caused by using cheap material. Never mind the grease paint, either. You—you won't always have to smear around in it—partner!"

While he hurried to make himself presentable, Gary's thoughts dwelt upon that word "partner" and the lingering sweetness of Patricia's tone. Patricia Connolly was not a feather-brained creature who would repeat parrotlike whatever phrase she happened to have heard and fancied. She did not run to second-hand superlatives. When she told Gary that she had a wonderful surprise for him, she would not, for instance, mean that she had done her hair in a new fashion or had bought a new record for the phonograph. And she had never before called him partner in any tone whatever. Gary would have remembered it if she had.

"What the heck is she going to spring on me *now?*" he kept wondering during the hour that intervened between the 'phone call and his entrance into the scrap of bungalow in a bepalmed court where Patricia had her milk and her mail delivered to the tiny front porch.

The extra fifteen minutes had not been spent in whipping the harsh-voiced tenant on the third floor; indeed, Gary had forgotten all about him the moment he hung up the receiver. One simply cannot annihilate all the men one abuses in the course of a day's strained living in Los Angeles or any other over-full city. Gary had been delayed first by the tenacity of the grease paint on his person, and after that by the heavy traffic on the street cars. Two cars had gone whanging past him packed solidly with peevish human beings and with men and boys clinging to every protuberance on the outside. When the third car stopped to let a clinging passenger drop off—shaking down his cuffs and flexing his cramped fingers—Gary had darted in like a hornet, seized toe-hold and finger-hold and hung on.

And so, fifteen minutes late, he arrived at Patricia's door and was let into Paradise and delectable odors and the presence of Patricia, who looked as though Christmas had come unexpectedly and she was waiting until the candles were lighted on the tree so she could present Gary with a million dollars. Her honest sweetness and her adorable little way of mothering Gary—though she was fours years younger—tingled with an air of holding back with difficulty the news of some amazing good fortune.

Patricia shared the bungalow with a trained nurse who was usually absent on a "case", so that Patricia was practically independent and alone. Most girls of twenty couldn't have done it and kept their mental balance; but Patricia was herself under any and all conditions, and it did not seem strange for her to be living alone the greater part of the time. Freedom, to her, spelled neither license nor loneliness; she lived as though her mother were always in the next room. Patricia felt sometimes that her mother was closer, very close beside her. It made her happier to feel so, but never had it made her feel ashamed.

She had evolved the dinner in this manner: while her boss was keeping her waiting until he had refreshed his memory of a certain special price on alfalfa molasses and oil cakes, etc., etc., in carload and half-carload lots, Patricia had jotted down in good shorthand, "chicken, about two pounds with yellow legs and a limber wishbone or nothing doing; cost a dollar, I expect—is Gary worth it? I'll say he is. God love ums. Strawberries, two boxes—Hood Rivers, if possible—try the City Market. Celery—if there's any that looks decent; if not, then artichokes or asparagus—Gary likes asparagus best—says he eats artichokes because it's fun—Dear Sir:—In response to your favor of the 17th inst.,—" and so on.

Some girls would have quoted asparagus in carload lots, transcribing from such notes, and would have put alfalfa molasses on the dinner menu; but not Patricia.

On her way home from the office in the dusty, humming barn of a building that housed the grain milling company which supported her in return for faithful service rendered, Patricia shopped at the big City Market where the sales people all had tired eyes and mechanical smiles, and a general air of hopelessly endeavoring to please every one so that no harassed marketers would complain to the manager. Patricia made her purchases as painless to the sales girl as possible, knowing too well what that strained smile meant. The great market buzzed like a bee-tree when you strike its trunk with a club.

She bought a manila paper shopping bag, but her packages overflowed the bag, so that she carried the two boxes of strawberries in her hand, and worried all the way home for fear the string would break; and held the warm tea biscuits under her arm, protecting them as anxiously as a hen protects her covered chicks. By prodding with her elbows and bracing her feet against the swaying crush, and giving now and then a haughty stare, Patricia achieved the miracle of arriving at Rose Court with her full menu and only one yellow leg of the chicken protruding stiffly from its wrappings.

She dumped her armload on the table in the kitchenette and rushed out again to buy flowers from the vendor who was chanting his wares half a block away. She was tingling all over with nerve weariness, yet she could smile brightly at the Greek so that he went on with a little glow of friendliness toward the world. At the rose-arched entrance to the Court she tilted her wrist, looked at her watch and said, "Good Lord! That late?" and dashed up to her door like a maiden pursued.

Yet here she was at seven, in a cool little pansy-tinted voile, dainty and serene as any young hostess in Westmoreland Place half a mile away. Even the strawberry stain on her finger tips could easily be mistaken for the new fad in manicuring. Can you wonder that Gary forgot every disagreeable thing he ever knew—including frowsy, unhomelike bachelor quarters, crowded street cars, all the petty aches and ills of movie work—when he unfolded his napkin and looked across the table at Patricia?

"Coffee now, or with dessert? Gary, don't you dare look question marks at me! I can't have your mind distracted with food while I'm telling you the most wonderful thing in the world. Moreover, this dinner deserves a little appreciation." Patricia's lips trembled, but only because she was tired and excited and happy. Her happiness would have been quite apparent to a blind man.

I do not mean to hint that Patricia deliberately fed Gary to repletion with the things he liked best, before imparting her *won*-derful surprise. She had frequently cooked nice little dinners for him when there was nothing surprising to follow. But it is a fact that when she had stacked the dishes neatly away for a later washing, and returned the dining table to its ordinary library-table guise, Gary looked as if nothing on earth could disturb him. Mental, emotional and physical content permeated the atmosphere of his immediate neighborhood. Patricia sat down and laid her arms upon the table, and studied Gary, biting her lips to hide their quiver.

CHAPTER TWO
PATRICIA EXPLAINS

Womanlike, Patricia began in a somewhat roundabout fashion and in a tone not far from cajolery.

"Gary! You do know all about ranch life and raising cattle and hay and horses and so on, don't you?"

Gary was lighting a cigarette. If he had learned the "picture value" of holding a pose, he was at least unconscious of his deliberation in waving out the match flame before he replied. His was a profile very effective in close-ups against the firelight. Holding a pose comes to be second nature to an actor who has to do those things for a living.

"Dad would rather feature the so-on stuff. Subtitle, father saying, 'You ain't much on raisin' cattle but you're shore an expert at raisin' hell!' Cut back to son on horse at gate, gazing wistfully toward house. Sighs. Turns away. Iris out, son riding away into dusk. Why?"

"Fathers are like that. Of course you know all about those things. You were raised on a ranch. Have you landed that contract with Mills yet, to play Western leads?"

"Not yet—Mills is waiting for his chief to come on from New York. He's due here about the First. I was talking with Mills to-day, and he says he's morally certain they'll give me a company of my own and put on Western Features. You know what that would mean, Pat—a year's contract for me. And we could get married——"

"Yes, never mind that, since you haven't landed it." Patricia drew in her breath. "Well, you know what I think of the movie game; we've thrashed that all out, times enough. I simply can't see *my* husband making movie love to various and sundry females who sob and smile and smirk at him for so many dollars per. We'll skip that. Also my conviction that the movies are lowering—cheapening to any full-sized man. Smirking and frowning before a camera, and making mushy love for kids on the front seats to stamp and whistle at—well, never mind; we won't go into that at this time.

"You know, Gary. I just love you to be Western; but I want you to be *real* Western—my own range hero. Not cheap, movie make-believe. I want you to get out and live the West. I can close my eyes and see you on a cattle ranch, riding out at dawn after your own cattle—doing your part in increasing the world's production of food—being something big and really worth while!"

"Can you? You're a good little seer, Pat. Golly, grandma! I wish I'd saved half of that shortcake to eat after a while. Now I'm so full I can't swallow a mouthful of smoke. What's the surprise, kid? Don't hold the suspense till the interest flags—that's bad business. Makes the story drag."

"Why, I'm telling you, Gary!" Patricia opened her eyes at him in a way that would have brought any movie queen a raise in salary. "It's just that you're going to have a chance to live up to what's really in you. You're going to manage a cattle ranch, dear. Not a real big one—yet. But you'll have the fun of seeing it grow."

"Oh-ah-h—I'll have the fun—er-r—all right, Pat, *I* give it up." Gary settled back again with his head against the cushion "Tell us the joke. My brain's leather to-night; had a heck of a day."

"The joke? Why, the joke is—well, just that you don't get it! I knew you wouldn't, just at first. Think, Gary! Just close your eyes and think of miles and miles of open range and no fences, and herds of cattle roaming free. Picture a home ranch against the mountains, in a cañon called—let's play it's called Johnnywater. Are you doing it?"

"Uh-huh. I'm thinking——" But he sounded drowsy, as if he would be asleep presently if he continued holding his eyes shut. "Open range and cattle roaming free—there ain't no such animal."

"That's where the big surprise comes in, Gary. Listen. This is the most important thing that ever happened to either of us. I—I can hardly talk about it, it's so perfectly *wonderful*. You'd never guess in a million years. But I—well, read these papers, Gary boy—I'll explain them afterwards."

Gary opened his eyes somewhat reluctantly, smiled endearingly at the flushed Patricia and accepted two legal-looking documents which she proffered with what might almost have been termed a flourish. He glanced at them somewhat indifferently, glanced again, gave Patricia a startled look, and sat up as if some one had prodded him unexpectedly in the back. He read both papers through frowningly, unconsciously registering consternation. When he had finished, he stared blankly at Patricia for a full minute.

"Pat Connolly, what the heck is this trick deed? I can't feature it. I don't *get* it! What's the big idea?"

"That's just a deed, Gary. The cattle and the brand and the water right to Johnnywater Spring, and the squatter's right to the pasturage and improvements are all included—as you would have seen if you had read it carefully. The other paper is the water right, that he got from the State. Besides that, I have the affidavits of two men who swear that William Waddell legally owned one hundred head of cattle and the funny X brand, and that everything is all straight to the best of their knowledge and belief.

"I insisted upon the affidavits being furnished, since I couldn't afford to make a trip away up there myself. It's all right, Gary. I could send them all to jail for perjury and things of that sort if they have lied about it."

Patricia pressed her palms hard upon the table and gave a subdued little squeal of sheer ecstasy.

"Just think of it, Gary! After almost despairing of ever being able to have a ranch of our own, so that you could ride around and really manage things, instead of pretending it in pictures, Fate gave me this wonderful chance!

"I was working up our mailing list, and ran across an ad in the Tonopah paper, of this place for sale. The 'Free grazing and water rights in open range country' caught my eye first. And the price was cheap—scandalously cheap for a stock ranch. I answered the ad right away—that was over a month ago, Gary. I've kept it a secret, because I hate arguments so, and I knew you'd argue against it. Any, anyway," she added naïvely, "you've been away on location so I couldn't tell you.

"That country is all unsurveyed for miles and miles and *miles*. Mr. Waddell writes that there are absolutely no grazing restrictions whatever, and that even their saddle and work horses run loose the year around. He says the winters are open——"

That last bit of information was delivered somewhat doubtfully. Patricia had lived in Southern California since she was a tiny tot and did not know exactly what an "open" winter meant.

"It's scarcely settled at all, and there are no sheep in the country. I knew that would be important, so I asked, particularly. It's in a part of the country that has been overlooked, Mr. Waddell says, just because it's quite a long way from the railroad. I never dreamed there was any unsurveyed country left in America. Did you, Gary?"

Gary had slumped down in the big chair and was smoking his cigarette with thoughtful deliberation. His eyes veiled themselves before Patricia's glowing enthusiasm.

"Death Valley is unsurveyed," he observed grimly.

"I'm not talking about Death Valley," Patricia retorted impatiently. "I mean cattle range. I've been corresponding with Mr. Waddell for a month, so I have all the facts."

"*All* the facts, kid?" Gary was no fool. He was serious enough now, and the muscles along his jaw were hardening a little. His director would have been tickled with that expression for a close-up of slow-growing anger.

"The only country left unsurveyed to-day is desert that would starve a horn toad to death in a week. Some one has put one over on you, Pat. Where does he live? If you've paid him any money yet, I'll have to go and get it back for you. You've bought a gold brick, Pat."

"I have not! I investigated, I tell you. I have really bought the Waddell outfit—cattle, horses, brand, ranch, water rights and everything. It took all the insurance money dad left me, except just a few hundred dollars. That Power of Attorney—I pinned it on the back of the deed to surprise you, and you haven't looked at it yet—cost me ten dollars, Gary Marshall! It gives you the right to go over there and run the outfit and transact business just as if you were the owner. I—I thought you might need it, and it would be just as well to have it."

Gary leaned forward, his jaw squared, his right hand shut to a fighting fist on the table.

"Do you think for a minute I'm crazy enough to go over *there*? To quit a good job that's just opening up into something big, and go off in the sand somewhere to watch cattle starve to death? It just happens that I do know a little about the cow business. Cattle have to eat, my dear girl. They don't just walk around in front of a camera to give dolled-up cowboys a chance to ride. They require food occasionally.

"Why, Pat, take a look at that deed! That in itself ought to have been enough to warn you. It's recorded in Tonopah. *Tonopah!* I was there on location once when we made *The Gold Boom*. It's a mining town—not a cow town, Pat."

Patricia smiled patiently.

"I know it, Gary. I didn't say that Johnnywater lies inside the city limits of Tonopah. Mines and cattle are not like sheep and cattle; they don't clash. There are cattle all around in that country." Patricia swept out an arm to indicate vast areas. "We have inquiries from cattle men all over Nevada about stock food. I've billed out alfalfa molasses and oil cakes to several Nevada towns. And remember, I was making up a mailing list for our literature when I ran across the ad. We don't mail our price lists to milliners, either. They raise cattle all through that country."

"Well, *I* don't raise 'em there—that's flat." Gary settled back in his chair with absolute finality in tone, words and manner.

"Then I'm a ruined woman." But Patricia said it calmly, even with a little secret satisfaction. "I shall have to go myself, then, and run the ranch, and get killed by bronks and bitten to death by Gila monsters and carried off by the Indians——"

"Piffle!" from the big chair. "You couldn't get on a bronk that was dangerous, and Gila monsters live farther south, and the Injuns are too lazy to carry anybody off. Besides, I wouldn't let you go."

"Then I'm still a ruined woman, except that I'm ruined quicker. My cows will die and my calves will be rustled and my horses ridden off—*my* cows and *my* calves and *my* horses!"

"Sell!" shouted Gary, forgetting other Bungalow Courters in his sudden fury. "You're stung, I tell you. Sell the damned thing!"

Patricia looked at him. She had a pretty little round chin, but there were times when it squared itself surprisingly. And whenever it did square itself, you could souse Patricia and hold her head under water until air bubbles ceased to rise; and if you brought her up and got her gasping again, Patricia would gasp, "Scissors!" like the old woman in the story.

"No. I shall not sell. I shall not do anything more than I have done already. If you refuse to go to Nevada and take charge of Johnnywater, I shall go myself or I shall let my cattle starve."

She would, too. Gary knew that. He looked steadily at her until he was sure of the square chin and all, and then he threw out both hands as if in complete surrender.

"Oh, very well," he said tolerantly. "We won't quarrel about it, Pat."

CHAPTER THREE
PATRICIA TAKES HER STAND

A young man of intelligence may absorb a great many psychological truths while helping to build in pictures mock dramas more or less similar to real, human problems. Gary wore a brain under his mop of brown hair, and he had that quality of stubbornness which will adopt strategy—guile, even—for the sake of winning a fight. To-night, he chose to assume the air of defeat that he might win ultimate victory.

Gary had not the slightest intention of ruining his own future as well as Patricia's by yielding with an easy, "Oh, very well" surrender, and going away into the wilds of Nevada to attempt the raising of cattle in a district so worthless that it had never so much as seen a surveyor's transit. Desert it must be; a howling waste of sand and lizards and snakes. The very fact that Patricia had been able, with a few thousands of dollars, to buy out a completely equipped cattle ranch, damned the venture at once as the mad freak of a romantic girl's ignorance. He set himself now to the task of patiently convincing Patricia of her madness.

Patricia, however, was not to be convinced. For every argument of Gary's she found another to combat it. She repeated more than once the old range slogan that you simply can't lose money in cattle. She told Gary that here was an opportunity, sent by a watchful Providence, for him to make good in a really worth-while business; and urged upon him the theory that pioneering brings out the best qualities in a man.

She attacked furiously Gary's ambition to become a screen star, reminding him how cheap and paltry is that success which is based only upon a man's good looks; and how easily screen stars fall meteorically into the hopeless void of forgotten favorites.

"It isn't just that I've dreamed all my life of owning cattle and living away out in the wilderness," she finished, with reddened cheeks and eyes terribly in earnest. "I know the fine mettle you're made of, Gary, and I couldn't see it spoiled while they fed your vanity at the studios.

"I had the money to buy this cattle ranch at Johnnywater—but of course I knew that I should be perfectly helpless with it alone. I don't know the business of raising cattle, except that I know the most popular kinds of stock food and the prices and freight rates to various points. But you were born on a cattle ranch, Gary, and I knew that you could make a success of it. I knew that you could go and take charge of the ranch, and put the investment on a paying basis; which is a lot better than just leaving that money in the bank, drawing four and a half per cent. And I'll go on with the milling company until the ranch is on its feet. My salary can go into what improvements are necessary. It's an ideal combination, I think."

She must have felt another argument coming to speech behind Gary's compressed lips; for she added, with a squared chin to give the statement force,

"This isn't threatening—a threat is always a sign of conscious weakness. I merely wish to make the statement that unless you go over and take charge of the Johnnywater ranch, I shall go myself. I absolutely *refuse* to sell. I don't know anything about running a ranch, and I was never on a horse in my life, so I'd undoubtedly make a beautiful mess of it. But I should have to tackle it, just the same; because I really can't afford to positively throw away five thousand dollars, you know. I should have to make some attempt to save it, at least. When I failed—as I probably should—I'd have to go away somewhere and get a job I hated, and develop into a sour old maid. Because, Gary, if you flatly refused to take charge over there, as you *threaten* to do, we certainly couldn't marry and expect to live together happily with Johnnywater ranch as a skeleton in our closet.

"So that's where I stand, Gary. Naturally, the prospect doesn't appeal to you at this moment. You're sitting here in a big, overstuffed chair, fed on good things, with a comfy cushion behind your shoulders and a shaded light over your head. You look very handsome indeed—and you know it just as well as I do. You are perfectly aware of the fact that this would make a stunning close-up of you—with the camera set to show your profile and that heart-disturbing wave over your right temple.

"Just at this minute you don't particularly care about sitting on a wooden chair in a cabin away out in the wilderness, hearing coyotes howl on a hill and your saddle horses champing hay in a sod-roofed stable, and you thinking how it's miles to the nearest neighbor—and an audience! You've reached the point, Gary, where a little mental surgery is absolutely necessary to your future mental health. I can see that your soul is beginning to show symptoms of going a tiny bit flabby. And I simply *loathe* flabby-souled men with handsome faces and shoulders as broad as yours!"

That was like jabbing Gary in the back with a hatpin. He sat up with a jerk.

"Flabby-souled! Good Lord, Pat! Why pile up the insults? This is getting good, I must say!" He leaned back in the chair again, the first effect of the jab having passed. "I can stand all this knocking the movie game—I'm used to it, heck knows. I might just point out, however, that making a living by expressing the emotions of men in stories is no worse than pounding a typewriter for a living. What's the difference whether you sell your profile or your fingers? And what do you think——"

"I think it's ten o'clock, Gary Marshall, and I've said what I have to say and there's no argument, because I simply won't argue. I suppose you'll need sleep if you still have to be at the studio at seven o'clock in the morning so that you can get into your painted eyebrows and painted eyelashes and painted lips for the day's smirk."

Gary heaved himself out of his chair and reached for his hat, forgetting to observe subconsciously how effectively he did it. Patricia's mental surgery had driven the lance deep into his pride and self-esteem, which in a handsome young man of twenty-four is quite as sensitive to pain as an eyeball. Patricia had omitted the mental anesthetic of a little flattery, and she had twisted the knife sickeningly. Painted eyelashes and painted lips nauseated Gary quite suddenly; but scarcely more than did the thought of that ranch of a hundred cattle in a Nevada desert, which Patricia had beggared herself to buy.

"Well, good night, Pat. I must be going. Awfully pleasant evening—great little dinner and all that. I wish you all kinds of luck with your cattle ranch. 'Bye."

Patricia did not believe that he would go like that. She thought he was merely bluffing. She did not so much as move a finger until he had shut the door rather decisively behind him and she heard his feet striking firmly on the cement walk that led to the street.

A slight chill of foreboding quivered along her spine as the footsteps sounded fainter and fainter down the pavement. She had known Gary Marshall for three years and had worn a half-carat diamond for six months. She had argued with him for hours; they had quarreled furiously at times, and he had registered anger, indignation, arrogance and hurt pride in several effective forms. But she had never before seen him behave in just this manner.

Of course he would hate that little slam of hers about the paint and the profile, she told herself hearteningly. She had struck deliberately at his pride and his vanity, though in justice she was compelled to confess to herself that Gary had very little vanity for a man so good-looking as he was. She had wanted him to hate what she said, so that he would be forced to give up the movie life which she hated. Still, his sudden going startled her considerably.

It occurred to her later that he had absent-mindedly carried off her papers. She remembered how he had stuffed them into his coat pocket—just as if they were his and didn't amount to much anyway—while the argument was going on. Well, since he had taken them away with him he would have to return them, no matter how mad he was; and in the meantime it might do him good to read them over again. He couldn't help seeing how she had burned her financial bridges behind her—for his sake.

Patricia brushed her eyes impatiently with her fingers and sighed. In a moment she pinned on an apron and attacked the dinner dishes savagely, wondering why women are such fools as to fall in love with a man, and then worry themselves into wrinkles over his shortcomings. Six months ago, Gary Marshall had not owned a fault to his name. Now, her whole heart was set upon eradicating faults which she had discovered.

"He shall *not* be spoiled—if I have to quarrel with him every day! There's something more to him than that mop of wavy brown hair that won't behave, and those straight eyebrows that won't behave either, but actually *talk* at you—and those eyes—— That darned leading girl can't make *me* believe it's all acting, when she rolls her eyes up at him and snuggles against his shoulder. That's *my* shoulder! And Gary says selling your profile is like selling your fingers! It might be—if the boss bought my fingers to *kiss*! And I don't care! It was positively indecent, the way Gary kissed that girl in his last picture. If he wasn't such a dear——"

Patricia snuffled a bit while she scraped chicken gravy off a plate. Gary's plate. "Let him sulk. He'll come back when he cools off. And he'll *have* to give in and go to Nevada. He'll never see me lose five thousand dollars. And those nasty little movie queens can find somebody else to roll up their eyes at. Oh, darn!"

CHAPTER FOUR
GARY GOES ON THE WARPATH

One thing which a motion-picture actor may not do and retain the tolerance of any one who knows him is to stop work in the middle of a picture. If there is an unforgivable sin in the movie world, that is it. Nevertheless, even sins called unforgivable may be condoned in certain circumstances; even the most stringent rules may be broken now and then, or bent to meet an individual need.

Gary spent a sleepless night wondering how he might with impunity commit the unforgivable sin. In spite of his anger at Patricia and his sense of her injustice, certain words of hers rankled in a way that would have pleased Patricia immensely, had she known it.

He rode out to the studio one car earlier than usual, and went straight to the little cubbyhole of a dressing room to put on his make-up as Chief Eagle Eye. Such was the force of Patricia's speech that Gary swore vaguely, at nothing in particular, while he painted his eyebrows, lashes and lips, and streaked the vermilion war paint down his cheeks. He scrubbed the copper-colored powder into the grease paint on his arms and chest, still swearing softly and steadily in a monotonous undertone that sounded, ten feet away, like a monk mumbling over his beads.

With the help of a fellow actor he became a noble red man from the scalp lock to his waist, got into fringed buckskin leggings, lavishly feathered war bonnet, some imitation elk-tooth necklaces and beaded moccasins. Then, with his quiver full of arrows (poisoned in the sub-titles) slung over his painted shoulders, and the mighty bow of Chief Eagle Eye in his hand, Gary stalked out into the lot in search of the director, Mills.

When one knows his director personally as a friend, one may, if he is a coming young star and not too insufferably aware of his starlike qualities, accomplish much in the way of emergency revisions of story and stringent rules.

Wherefore, to the future amazement of the author, Chief Eagle Eye that day died three different deaths, close up in front of two grinding cameras; though Chief Eagle Eye had not been expected to die at all in the picture. The director stood just behind the camera, his megaphone under his arm, his hands on his hips, his hat on the back of his head and a grin on his perspiring face.

"Thattaboy, Gary! Just sag at the knees and go down slowly, as you try to draw the bow. That's it—try to get up—well, that's good business, trying to shoot from the ground! Now try to heave yourself up again—just lift your body, like your legs is paralyzed—shot in the back, maybe. All right—that's great stuff. Now rouse yourself with one last effort—lift your head and chant the death song! Gulp, man!

"Run in there, Bill—you're horrified. Try to lift him up and drag him back out of danger. Say! Wince, man, like you're shot through the lungs—no, *I meant Gary!*—well, damn it, let it go—but how-the-hell-do-you-expect-to-drag-a-man-off-when-you've-got-a-slug-in-your-*lungs*? You acted like some one had stuck you with a pin! Git outa the scene—Gary's doing the dying, you ain't!—— *Cut*—we'll have to do that over. A kid four years old would never stand for that damfool play.

"Now, Gary, try that again. Keep that business with the bow. And try and get that same vindictive look—you know, with your lips drawn back while you're trying to bend the bow and let fly one last arrow. This time you die alone. Can't have a death scene like that gummed up by a boob like Bill lopin' in and actin' like he'd sat on a bee—all right—come in—*camera*——

"That's fine—now take your time, take your time—now, as the bow sags—you're growing weaker—rouse yourself and chant your death song! That's the stuff! Lift your head—turn it so your profile shows" (Gary swore without moving his lips "—hold that, while you raise your hand palm out—peace greeting to your ancestors you see in the clouds! *Great!* H-o-o-l-d it—one—two—three—now-go-slack-all-at-once——*Cut!*"

Gary picked himself up, took off his war bonnet and laid it on a rock, reached into his wampum belt and produced a sack of Bull Durham and a book of papers. The director came over and sat down beside him, accepting the cigarette Gary had just rolled.

"Great scene, Gary. By gosh, that ought to get over big. When you get back, call me up right away, will you? I ought to know something definite next week, at the latest. Try and be here when Cohen gets here; I want you to meet him. By gosh, it's a crime not to give you a feature company. Well, have Mack drive you back in my car. You haven't any too much time."

That's what it means to have the director for your friend. He can draw out your scenes and keep you working many an extra week if you are hard up, or he can kill you off on short notice and let you go, if you happen to have urgent business elsewhere; and must travel from Toponga Cañon to the studio, take off your make-up—an ungodly, messy make-up in this case—pack a suit case, buy a ticket and catch the eight o'clock train that evening.

Gary, having died with much dignity and a magnificent profile in full view of future weeping audiences, was free from further responsibility toward the company and could go where he did not please. Which, of course, was Tonopah.

He was just boyish enough in his anger, hurt enough in his man's pride, to go without another word to Patricia. Flabby-souled, hunh? Painted eyebrows, painted lashes, painted lips—golly grandma! Pat surely could take the hide off a man, and smile while she did it!

He meant to take that Power of Attorney she had so naïvely placed in his hands, and work it for all there was in it. He meant to sell that gold brick of a "stock ranch" Waddell had worked off on her, and lick Waddell and the two men who had signed affidavits for him. He meant to go back, then, and give Pat her money, and tell her for the Lord's sake to have a little sense, and put her five thousand dollars in a trust fund, where she couldn't get hold of it for the first faker that came along and held out his hand. After that—Gary was not sure what he would do. He was still very angry with Patricia; but after he had asserted his masculine authority and proved to her that the female of our species is less intelligent than the male, it is barely possible that he might forgive the girl.

CHAPTER FIVE
GARY DOES A LITTLE SLEUTHING

Tonopah as a mining town appealed strongly to Gary's love of the picturesque. Tonopah is a hilly little town, with a mine in its very middle, and with narrow, crooked streets that slope steeply and take sharp turnings. Houses perched on knobs of barren, red earth, or clung precariously to steep hillsides. The courthouse, a modern, cement building with broad steps flanked by pillars, stood with aloof dignity upon a hill that made Gary puff a little in the climbing.

On the courthouse steps he finished his cigarette before going inside, and stood gazing at the town below him and at the barren buttes beyond. As far as he could see, the world was a forbidding, sterile world; unfriendly, inhospitable—a miserly world guarding jealously the riches deep-hidden within its hills. When he tried to visualize range cattle roaming over those hills, Gary's lips twisted contemptuously.

He turned and went in, his footsteps clumping down the empty, echoing corridor to the office of the County Recorder. A wholesome-looking girl with hair almost the color of Patricia's rose from before a typewriter and came forward to the counter. Her eyes widened a bit when she looked at Gary, and the color deepened a little in her cheeks. Perhaps she had seen Gary's face on the screen and remembered it pleasantly; certainly a man like Gary Marshall walks but seldom into the Recorder's office of any desert county seat. Gary told her very briefly what he wanted, and the County Recorder herself came forward to serve him.

Very obligingly she looked up all the records pertaining to Johnnywater. Gary himself went in with her to lift the heavy record books down from their places in the vault behind the office. The County Recorder was thorough as well as obliging. Gary lifted approximately a quarter of a ton of books, and came out of the vault wiping perspiration from inside his collar and smoothing his plumage generally after the exercise. It was a warm day in Tonopah.

Gary had not a doubt left to pin his hopes upon. The County Recorder had looked up water rights to Johnnywater and adjacent springs, and had made sure that Waddell had made no previous transfers to other parties, a piece of treachery which Gary had vaguely hoped to uncover. Patricia's title appeared to be dishearteningly unassailable. Gary would have been willing to spend his last dollar in prosecuting Waddell for fraud; but apparently no such villainy had brought Waddell within his clutches.

From the County Recorder, who had a warm, motherly personality and was chronically homesick for Pasadena and eager to help any one who knew the place as intimately as did Gary, he learned how great a stranger Tonopah is to her county corners. Pat was right, he discovered. Miles and miles of country lay all unsurveyed; a vast area to be approached in the spirit of the pioneer who sets out to explore a land unknown.

Roughly scaling the district on the county map which the Recorder borrowed from the Clerk (and which Gary promptly bought when he found that it was for sale) he decided that the water holes in the Johnnywater district were approximately twenty to forty miles apart.

"Pat's cows will have to pack canteens where village bossies wear bells on their lavallieres," Gary grinned to the County Recorder. "Calves are probably taboo in the best bovine circles of Nevada—unless they learn to ride to water on their mammas' backs, like baby toads."

The Recorder smiled at him somewhat wistfully. "You remind me of my son in Pasadena," she said. "He always joked over the drawbacks. I wish you were going to be within riding distance of here; I've an extra room that I'd love to have you use sometimes. But—" she sighed, "—you'll probably never make the trip over here unless you come the roundabout way on the train, to record something. And the mail is much more convenient, of course. What few prospectors record mining claims in that district nearly always send them by mail, I've noticed. In all the time I've been in office, this Mr. Waddell is the only man from that part of the county who came here personally. He said he had other business here, I remember, and intended going on East."

"So Waddell went East, did he?" Gary looked up from the map. "He's already gone, I suppose."

"I suppose so. I remember he said he was going to England to visit his old home. His health was bad, I imagine; I noticed he looked thin and worried, and his manner was very nervous."

"It ought to be," Gary mumbled over the map. "Isn't there any road at all, tapping that country from here?"

The Recorder didn't know, but she thought the County Clerk might be able to tell him. The County Clerk had been much longer in the country and was in close touch with the work of the commissioners. So Gary thanked her with his nicest manner, sent a vague smile toward the girl with hair like Patricia's, and went away to interview the County Clerk.

When he left the court house Gary had a few facts firmly fixed in his mind. He knew that Patricia's fake cattle ranch was more accessible to Las Vegas than to Tonopah. Furthermore, the men who had signed the affidavits vouching for Waddell did not belong in Tonopah, but could probably be traced from Las Vegas more easily. And there seemed no question at all of the legality of the transaction.

Gary next day retraced the miles halfway back to Los Angeles, waited for long, lonesome hours in a tiny desert station for the train from Barstow, boarded it and made a fresh start, on another railroad, toward Patricia's cattle ranch. So far he had no reason whatever for optimism concerning the investment. The best he could muster was a faint hope that some other trustful soul might be found with five thousand dollars, no business sense whatever and a hunger for story-book wilderness. Should such an improbable combination stray into Gary's presence before Patricia's Walking X cattle all starved to death, Gary promised himself grimly that he would stop at nothing short of a blackjack in his efforts to sell Johnnywater. He felt that Providence had prevailed upon Patricia to place that Power of Attorney in his hands, and he meant to use it to the limit.

In Las Vegas, where Gary continued his inquiries, he tramped here and there before he discovered any one who had ever heard of Johnnywater. One man knew Waddell slightly, and another was of the opinion that the two who had made affidavit for Waddell must live somewhere in the desert. This man suggested that Gary should stick around town until they came in for supplies or something. Gary snorted at that advice and continued wandering here and there, asking questions of garage men and street loiterers who had what he called the earmarks of the desert. One of these interrupted himself in the middle of a sentence, spat into the gutter and pointed.

"There's one of 'em, now. That's Monty Girard just turned the corner by the hotel. When he lights som'eres, you can talk to 'im. Like as not you can ride out with 'im to camp, if you got the nerve. Ain't many that has. I tried ridin' with 'im once for a mile, down here to the dairy, and I sure as hell feel the effects of it yet. Give me a crick in the back I never *will* git over. I'd ruther board a raw bronk any day than get in that Ford uh his'n. You go speak to Monty, mister. He can tell yuh more about what you want to know than any man in Vegas, I reckon."

Gary watched the man in the Ford go rattling past, pull up to the sidewalk in the next block and stop. He sauntered toward the spot. It was a day for sauntering and for seeking the shady side of the street; Monty Girard was leaving the post-office with a canvas bag in his hand when Gary met him. Gary was not in the mood for much ceremony. He stopped Girard in the middle of the sidewalk.

"I believe you signed an affidavit for a man named Waddell, in regard to the Johnnywater outfit. I'd like to have a few minutes' talk with you."

"Why, shore!" Monty Girard glanced down at the mail bag, stepped past Gary and tossed the bag into the back of his car. "Your name's Connolly, I guess. Going out to Johnnywater?"

Gary had not thought of friendliness toward any man connected with the Johnnywater transaction; yet friendliness was the keynote of Monty Girard's personality. The squinty wrinkles around his young blue eyes were not all caused by facing wind and sun; laughter lines were there, plenty of them. His voice, that suggested years spent in the southwest where men speak in easy, drawling tones, caressing in their softness, was friendliness itself; as was his quick smile, disclosing teeth as white and even as Gary himself could boast. In spite of himself, Gary's hostility lost its edge.

"If you haven't got your own car, you're welcome to ride out with me, Mr. Connolly. I'm going within fifteen miles of Johnnywater, and I can take yuh-all over as well as not."

Gary grinned relentingly.

"I came over to see how much of that outfit was faked," he said. "I'm not the buyer, but I have full authority to act for Pat Connolly. The deal was made rather—er—impulsively, and it is unfortunate that the buyer was unable to get over and see the place before closing the deal. Waddell has gone East, I hear. But you swore that things were as represented in the deal."

Monty Girard gave him one searching look from under the brim of his dusty, gray Stetson range hat. He looked down, absently reaching out a booted foot to shake a front wheel of his Ford.

"What I swore to was straight goods, all right. I figured that if Mr. Connolly was satisfied with the deal as it stood, it was no put-in of mine. I don't know of a thing that was misrepresented. Not if a man knows this country and knows what to expect."

"Now we're coming to the point, I think." Gary felt oddly that here was a man who would understand his position and perhaps sympathize with the task he had set himself to accomplish.

Monty Girard hesitated, looking at him inquiringly before he glanced up and down the street.

"Say, mister——"

"Marshall. Pardon me. Gary Marshall's my name."

"Well, Mr. Marshall, it's like this. I'm just in off a hundred-and-forty-mile drive—and it shore is hot from here to Indian. If you don't mind helpin' me hunt a cool spot, we'll have a near beer or something and talk this thing over."

Over their near beer Gary found the man he had intended to lick even more disarming. Monty Girard kept looking at him with covert intentness.

"Gary Marshall, you said your name was? I reckon yuh-all must be the fellow that done that whirlwind riding in a picture I saw, last time I was in town. I forget the name of it—but I shore don't forget the way yuh-all handled your hawse. A range rider gets mighty particular about the riding he sees in the movies. I'll bet yuh-all never learned in no riding school, Mr. Marshall; I'll bet another glass uh near beer you've rode the range some yourself."

"I was born on the Pecos," grinned Gary. "My old man had horses mostly; some cattle, of course. I left when I was eighteen."

"And that shore ain't been so many years it'd take all day to count 'em. Well, I shore didn't expect to meet that fellow I saw in the picture, on my next trip in to town."

Gary drank his beer slowly, studying Monty Girard. Somehow he got the impression that Girard did not welcome the subject of Johnnywater. Yet he had seemed sincere enough in declaring that he had told the truth in the affidavit. Gary pushed the glass out of his way and folded his arms on the table, leaning a little forward.

"Just where's the joker in this Johnnywater deal?" he asked abruptly. "There is one, isn't there?"

"Wel-l—you're going out there, ain't yuh?" Monty Girard hesitated oddly. "I don't know as there's any joker at all; not in the way yuh-all mean. It's a long ways off from the railroad, but Waddy wrote that in his letter to Mr. Connolly. I know that for a fact, because I read the letter. And uh course, cattle is down now—a man's scarcely got a livin' chance runnin' cattle, the way the market is now. But Mr. Connolly must uh known all that. The price Waddy put on the outfit could uh told 'im that, if nothin' else. I dunno as Waddy overcharged Connolly for the place. All depends on whether a man wanted to buy. Connolly did—I reckon. Leastways, he bought."

"Yes, I see your point. The deal was all right if a man wanted the place. But you're wondering what kind of a man would *want* the place. It's a lemon of some kind. That's about it—stop me if I'm wrong."

Monty Girard laughed dryly. "I'm mounted on a tired hawse, Mr. Marshall. I couldn't stop a run-down clock, and that's a fact."

"Well, I think I'll go out with you if you don't mind. I suppose I'll need blankets and a few supplies."

"Well, I reckon Waddy left pretty much everything he had out there. Soon as he got his money at the bank he fanned it for Merrie England. He just barely had a suit case when I saw him last. I reckon maybe yuh-all better take out a few things you'd hate to get along without. Flour, bacon an' beans you can pretty well count on. And, unless yuh-all want to take blankets of your own, you needn't be afraid to use Waddy's. Frank Waddell was shore a nice, clean housekeeper, and a nice man all around, only—kinda nervous."

Gary listened, taking it all in. His eyes, trained to the profession of putting emotions, thoughts, even things meant to be hidden, into the human face, so that all might see and read the meaning, watched Monty's face as he talked.

"Just what *is* it that made Waddell sell the Johnnywater ranch and clear out of the country?" he asked. "Just what makes you hate the place?"

Monty sent him a startled look.

"I never said I hated it," he parried. "It ain't anything to me, one way or the other."

"You *do* hate it. Why?"

"Wel-l—I dunno as I can hardly say. A man's got feelin's sometimes he can't hardly put into words. Lots of places in this country has got histories, Mr. Marshall. I guess—Johnnywater's all right. Waddy was a kind of nervous cuss."

CHAPTER SIX
JOHNNYWATER

Please do not picture a level waste of sand and scant sagebrush when you think of the Nevada desert. Barren it is, where water is not to be had; but level it is not, except where the beds of ancient lakes lie bare and yellow, hard as cement except when the rains soften the surface to sticky, red mud. Long mesas, with scattering clumps of greasewood and sage, lie gently tilted between sporadic mountain ranges streaked and scalloped with the varying rock formations that tell how long the world was in the making. Here and there larger mountains lift desolate barriers against the sky. Seen close, any part of the scene is somber at best. But distance softens the forbidding bleakness of the uplifted hummocks and crags, and paints them with magic lights and shadows.

In the higher altitudes the mountains are less bare; more friendly in a grim, uncompromising way and grown over scantily sometimes with piñons and juniper and the flat-leafed cedar whose wood is never too wet to burn with a great snapping, and is as likely to char temperamentally and go black. In these great buttes secret stores of water send little searching streams out through crevices among the rocks. Each cañon has its spring hidden away somewhere, and the water is clear and cold, stealing away from the melting snows on top.

A rough, little-used trail barely passable to a car, led into Johnnywater Cañon. To Gary the place was a distinct relief from the barren land that stretched between this butte and Las Vegas. The green of the piñon trees was refreshing as cool water on a hot day. The tiny stream that trickled over water-worn rocks in the little gully beside the cabin astonished him. For hours he had ridden through the parched waste land. For hours Monty had talked of scanty grazing and little water. In spite of himself, Gary's eyes brightened with pleasure when he first looked upon Johnnywater.

The sun still shone into the cañon, though presently it would drop behind the high shoulder of the butte. The little cabin squatting secretively between two tall piñons looked an ideal "set" for some border romance.

"It's not a bad-*looking* place," he commented with some reluctance. "Maybe Pat didn't pull such a boner after all." He climbed out of the car and walked toward the tiny stream. "Golly grandma, what's that! Chickens?"

"It shore enough is—but I kinda thought the coyotes and link-cats would of got all Waddy's chickens. He's been gone a week away."

"Good heck! I thought chickens liked to partake of a little nourishment occasionally. All the kinds I've met do."

Monty laughed lazily.

"Oh, Waddell he fixed a kind of feed box for 'em that lets down a few grains at a time. I reckon he filled it up before he went." Monty sent seeking glances into the undergrowth along the creek. "There ought to be a couple of shoats around here, too. And a cat."

Gary went into the cabin and stood looking around him curiously. Some attempt had been made to furnish the place with a few comforts, but the attempt had evidently perished of inanition. Flowered calico would have hidden the cubboard decently, had the curtains been clean. A box tacked against the wall held magazines and a book or two. The bunk was draped around the edge with the same flowered calico, with an old shoe protruding from beneath. One square window with a single sash looked down upon the little creek. Its twin looked down the cañon. Cast-off garments hung against the wall at the foot of the bunk.

"Great interior set for a poverty scene," Gary decided, rolling himself a smoke. "I don't intend to stay out on this location, you know. I'm here to sell the damned place. What's the quickest way to do that—quietly? I mean, without advertising it."

Monty Girard turned slowly and stared.

"There ain't no quick way," he said finally. "Waddy, he's been tryin' for three months to sell it—advertisin' in all the papers. He was in about as much of a hurry as a man could get in—and he was just about at the point where he was goin' to walk off and leave it, when this Mr. Connolly bit."

"Bit?"

"Bought. Yuh-all must have misunderstood."

"Either way, I don't feature it." Gary lighted the cigarette thoughtfully. "It looks a pretty fair place—for a hermit, or a man that's hiding out. What did this man Waddell buy it for? And how long ago?"

"I reckon he thought he wanted it. A couple of years ago, I reckon he aimed to settle down here."

"Well, why the heck didn't he do it then?" Gary sat down on the edge of the table and folded his arms. "Spread 'em out on the table, Monty. I won't shoot."

"You say yuh-all don't aim to stay here?" Monty leveled a glance at him.

"Not any longer than it takes to sell out. You look like a live wire. I'm going to appoint you my agent and see if you can't rustle a buyer—*quick*. I'll go back with you, when you go. That will be in a couple of days, you said. So tell me the joke, Monty. I asked you in town, yesterday, and you didn't do it."

"I can't say as I rightly know. I reckon maybe it was Waddy himself that was wrong, and nothin' the matter with Johnnywater. He got along all right here for awhile—but I guess he got kind of edgey, livin' alone here so much. He got to kinda imaginin' he was seein' things. And along last spring he got to hearin' 'em. So then he wanted to sell out right away quick."

"Oh." Gary sounded rather crestfallen. "A nut, hunh? I thought there was something faked about the place itself."

"Yuh-all read what I swore to," Monty reminded him with a touch of dignity. "I wouldn't help nobody fake a deal; not even a fellow in the shape Waddy was in. He had his money in here, and he had to git it out before he could leave. At that, he sold out at a loss. This is a right nice little place, Mr. Marshall, for anybody that wants a place like this."

"But you don't, hunh? Couldn't you buy the cattle?"

Monty shook his head regretfully.

"No, I couldn't. I couldn't buy out the Walkin' X brand now at a dime a head, and that's a fact. Cattle's away down. I'm just hangin' on, Mr. Marshall, and that's the case with every cattle owner in the country. It ain't my put-in, maybe, but if Johnnywater was mine, I know what I'd do."

"Well, let's hear it."

"Well, I'd fix things up best I could around here, and hang on to it awhile till times git better. Waddell asked seven thousand at first—and it'd be worth that if there was any market at all for cattle. Up the cañon here a piece, Waddy's got as pretty a patch of alfalfa as you'd want to look at. And a patch of potatoes that was doing fine, the last I see of 'em. He was aimin' to put the whole cañon bottom into alfalfa; and that's worth money in this country, now I'm tellin' yuh.

"Yuh see, Johnnywater's different from most of these cañons. It's wider and bigger every way, and it's got more water. A man could hang on to his cattle, and by kinda pettin' 'em along through the winter, and herdin' 'em away from the loco patches in the spring, he could make this a good payin' investment. That's what I reckoned this Mr. Connolly aimed to do."

"Pat Connolly bought this place," said Gary shortly, "because it sounded nice in the ad. It was a nut idea from the start. I'm here to try and fish the five thousand up out of the hole."

"Well, I reckon maybe that same ad would sound good to somebody else," Monty ventured.

But Gary shook his head. Since Patricia made up her mailing lists from the newspapers, Gary emphatically did not want to advertise.

They ended by cooking late dinner together, frying six fresh eggs which Gary discovered in the little dugout chicken house. After which Monty Girard unloaded what supplies Gary had brought, smoked a farewell cigarette and drove away to his own camp twenty miles farther on.

"It's a great life if you don't weaken," Gary observed tritely. "I might get a kick out of this, if Pat hadn't been so darned fresh about the movies, and so *gol-*darned stubborn about me camping here and doing the long-haired hick act for the rest of my life."

He went away then to hunt for the chicken feed; found it in another dugout cellar, and fed the chickens that came running hysterically out of the bushes when Gary rattled the pan and called them as he had seen gingham-gowned ingénues do in rural scenes.

"Golly grandma! If I could catch a young duck now, and cuddle it up under my dimpled chin, I'd make a swell Mary Pickford close-up," he chuckled to himself. "Down on the farm, by gum! *'Left the town to have some fun, and I'm a goin' to have some, yes, by gum!'* Pat Connolly's going to do some plain and fancy knuckling under, to pay for this stunt. Gosh, and there's the cat!"

CHAPTER SEVEN
THE VOICE

Gary got up from his chair three separate times to remove the lamp chimney (using a white cambric handkerchief to protect his manicured fingers from blisters). In the beginning, the flame had flourished two sharp points that smoked the chimney. After the third clipping it had three, and one of them was like a signal smoke in miniature.

Gary eyed it disgustedly while he filled his pipe. Smoking a pipe while he dreamed in the fire glow had made so popular a close-up of Gary Marshall that he had used the pose in his professional photographs and had, to date, autographed and mailed sixty-seven of the firelight profiles to sixty-seven eager fans. Nevertheless, he forgot that he had a profile now.

"Hunh! Pat ought to get a real kick out of this scene," he snorted. "Interior cabin—sitting alone—lifts head, listens. Sub-title: THE MOURNFUL HOWL OF THE COYOTE COMES TO HIM MINGLED WITH THE SOUND OF HORSES CHAMPING HAY. Only there ain't no horses, and if there were they wouldn't champ. Only steeds do that—in hifalutin', goldarned poetry. Pat ought to take a whirl at this Johnnywater stuff, herself. About twenty-four hours of it. It might make a different girl of her. Give her some sense, maybe."

Slowly his pessimistic glance went around the meager rectangle of the cabin. Think of a man holding up here for two years! "No wonder he went out of here a nut," was Gary's brief summary. "And it's my opinion the man's judgment had begun to skid when he bought the place. Good Lord! Why, he'd probably *seen* it before he paid down the money! He was a tough bird, if you ask me, to hang on for two years."

Gary's pipe, on its way to his lips that had just blown out a small, billowy cloud of smoke, stopped halfway and was held there motionless. His whole face stilled as his mind concentrated upon a sound.

"That's no coyote," he muttered, and listened again.

He got up and opened the door, leaning out into the starlight, one hand pressed against the rough-hewn logs of cedar. He listened again, turning his head slightly to determine the location of the sound.

A wind from the west, flowing over the towering butte, shivered the tops of the piñons. A gust it was, that died as it had been born, suddenly. As it lessened Gary heard distinctly a far-off, faint halloo.

"Hello!" he called back, stepping down upon the flat rock that formed the doorstep. "What's wanted? *Hello!*"

"'Il-*oo-ooh!*" cried the voice, from somewhere beyond the creek.

"*Hello!*" shouted Gary, megaphoning with his cupped palms. Some one was lost, probably, and had seen the light in the cabin.

Again the voice replied. It seemed to Gary that the man was shouting some message; but distance blurred the words so that only the cadence of the voice reached his ears.

Gary cupped his hands again and replied. He went down to the little creek and stood there listening, shouting now and then encouragement to the man on the bluff. He must be on the bluff, or at least far up its precipitous slope; for beyond the stream the trees gave way to bowlders, and above the bowlders rough outcroppings in ledge formation made steep scrambling. The top of the bluff was guarded by a huge rampart of solid rock; a "rim-rock" formation common throughout the desert States.

Gary tried to visualize that sheer wall of rock as he had seen it before dark. Without giving it much thought at the time, he somehow took it for granted that the cañon wall on that side was absolutely impassable. Still, there might be a trail to the top through some crevice invisible from below.

"Gosh, if a fellow's hurt up there, I'll have a merry heck of a time getting him down in the dark!" Gary told the mottled cat with one blue eye, that rubbed against his ankle. "There ought to be a lantern hanging somewhere. Never saw an interior cabin set in my life where a tin lantern didn't register."

He found the lantern, but it had no wick. Gary spent a profane fifteen minutes holding the smoky lamp in one hand and searching a high, littered shelf with the other, looking for lantern wicks. That he actually found one at last, tucked into a tomato can among some bolts and nails, seemed little short of a miracle. He had to rob the lamp of oil, because he did not know where Waddell kept his supply. Then the wick was a shade too wide, and Gary was obliged to force it through the burner with the point of his knife. When he finally got the lantern burning it was more distressingly horned than the lamp, and the globe immediately began an eclipse on one side. But Gary only swore and wiped his smeared fingers down his trousers, man-fashion.

Almost constantly the voice had called to him from the bluff. Gary went out and shouted that he was coming, and crossed the creek, the mottled cat at his heels. Gary had never been friendly toward cats, by the way; but isolation makes strange companions sometimes between animals and men, and Gary had already made friends with this one. He even waited, holding the lantern while the cat jumped the creek, forgetting it could see in the dark.

He made his way through the bushy growth beyond the stream, and scrambled upon a huge bowlder, from where he could see the face of the bluff. He stood there listening, straining his eyes into the dark.

The voice called to him twice. A wailing, anxious tone that carried a weight of trouble.

Gary once more megaphoned that he was coming, and began to climb the bluff, the smoking lantern swinging in his hands (a mere pin-prick of light in the surrounding darkness), the mottled cat following him in a series of leaps and quick rushes.

The lamp had gone out when Gary returned to the cabin. The lantern was still smoking vilely, with fumes of gas. Gary put the lantern on the table and sat down, wiping his face and neck with his handkerchief. The mottled cat crouched and sprang to his knee, where it dug claws to hang on and began purring immediately.

For an hour Gary had not heard the voice, and he was worried. Some one must be hurt, up there in the rocks. But until daylight came to his assistance Gary was absolutely helpless. He looked at his watch and saw that he had been stumbling over rocks and climbing between bowlders until nearly midnight. He had shouted, too, until his throat ached.

The man had answered, but Gary had never been able to distinguish any words. Always there had been that wailing note of pain, with now and then a muffled shriek at the end of the call. High up somewhere on the bluff he was, but Gary had never seemed able to come very close. There were too many ledges intervening. And at last the voice had grown fainter, until finally it ceased altogether.

"We'll have to get out at daylight and hunt him up," he said to the cat. "I can't feature this mountain goat stuff in the dark. But nobody could sit still and listen to that guy hollering for help. It'll be a heck of a note if he's broken a leg or something. That's about what happened—simplest thing in the world to break legs in that rock pile."

He stroked the cat absent-mindedly, holding himself motionless now and then while he listened. After awhile he put the cat down and went to bed, his thoughts clinging to the man who had called down from the bluff.

CHAPTER EIGHT
"THE CAT'S GOT 'EM TOO!"

Monty Girard did not return on the second day. A full week dragged itself minute by minute across Johnnywater; days began suddenly with a spurt of color over the eastern rim of the cañon, snailed it across the blue space above and after an interminable period ended in a red riot beyond the western rim, letting night flow into the cañon.

The first day went quickly enough. At sunrise Gary and the spotted cat searched the bluff where the voice had called beseechingly in the night. Gary carried a two-quart canteen filled with water, knowing that a man who has lain injured all night will have a maddening thirst by morning.

At noon he sat on a bowlder just under the rim rock, helped himself to a long drink from the canteen and stared disheartened down into the cañon. He was hoarse from shouting, but not so much as a whisper had he got in reply. The spotted cat had given up in disgust long ago and gone off on business of her own. He was willing to swear that he had covered every foot of that hillside, and probably he had, very nearly. And he had found no trace of any man, living or dead.

He slid off the bowlder and went picking his way down the steep bluff to the cabin. A humane impulse had sent him out as soon as he opened his eyes that morning. He was half-starved and more nearly exhausted than he had ever been after a hard day's work doing "stunts" for the movies.

Now and then he looked up the cañon to where Pat's alfalfa field lay, a sumptuous patch of deep green, like an emerald set deep in some dull metal. Nearer the cabin were the rows of potato plants which Monty had mentioned. There was a corral, too, just beyond a clump of trees behind the cabin. And from the head of the cañon to the mouth he could glimpse here and there the twisted thread of Johnnywater Creek.

By the time he had cooked and eaten breakfast and lunch together, and had fed the chickens, and located the whereabouts of two pigs whose grunting came to him from the bushes, the afternoon was well gone. And, on the whole, it had not gone so badly; except that he rather resented his fruitless search for a man who had shouted in the night and then disappeared.

"Drunk, maybe," Gary finally dismissed the subject from his mind. "He sure as heck couldn't be hurt so bad, if he was able to get out of the cañon in the dark. It'll be something to tell about when I get back. I'll ask Monty what he thinks about it, to-morrow."

But he didn't ask Monty. He rather expected that Monty would be along rather early in the forenoon, and he was ready by nine o'clock. He had filled the feed box for the chickens, had given the cat a farewell talk, and locked his pyjamas into his suit case. The rest of the day he spent in waiting.

One bit of movie training helped him now. By the time an actor has reached stardom, he knows how to sit and wait; doing nothing, thinking nothing in particular, gossiping a little, perhaps, but waiting always. Gary had many a time sat around killing time for hours at a stretch, that he might work for fifteen minutes on a scene. Waiting for Monty, then, was not such a hardship that second day.

But when the third day and the fourth and the fifth had gone, Gary began to register impatience and concern. He walked down the cañon and out upon the trail as far as was practical, half hoping that he might see some chance traveler. But the whole world seemed to be empty and waiting, with a still patience that placed no limit upon its quiescent expectancy.

Steeped in that desert magic which makes beautiful all distances, the big land shamed him somehow and sent him back into the cañon in a better frame of mind. Any trivial thing could have delayed Monty Girard. It was slightly comforting to know that the big world out there was smiling under the sky.

He was sitting at supper just after sundown that evening when a strange thing happened. The spotted cat—Gary by this time was calling her Faith because of her trustful disposition—was squatted on all fours beside the table, industriously lapping a saucer of condensed milk. For the want of more human companionship, Gary was joking with the cat, which responded now and then with a slight wave of her tail.

"You're the only thing I like about the whole darn outfit," Gary was saying. "I don't remember your being mentioned in the deed, so I think I'll just swipe you when I go. As a souvenir. Only I don't know what the heck I'll do with you—give you to Pat, I reckon."

Faith looked up with an amiable mew, but she did not look at Gary. Had a person been standing near the foot of the bunk six feet or so away, she would have been looking up into his face. She went back to lapping her milk, but Gary eyed her curiously. There was something odd about that look and that friendly little remark of hers, but for the life of him he could not explain just what was wrong.

Once again, while Gary watched her, the cat looked up at that invisible point the height of a man from the floor. She finished her milk, licked her lips satisfiedly and got up. She glanced at Gary, glanced again toward the bunk, arched her back, walked deliberately over and curved her body against nothing at all, purring her contented best.

Gary watched her with a contraction of the scalp on the back of his head. Faith stood there for a moment rubbing her side against empty air, looked up inquiringly, came over and jumped upon Gary's knee. There she tucked her feet under her, folded her tail close to her curiously mottled fur and settled herself for a good, purry little nap. Now and then she opened her eyes to look toward the bunk, her manner indifferent.

"The cat's got 'em, too," Gary told himself—but it is significant that he did not speak the words aloud as he had been doing those five days, just to combat the awful stillness of the cañon.

He stared intently toward the place where the cat had stood arching her body and purring. There was nothing there, so far as Gary could see. But slowly, as he stared toward the place, a mental picture formed in his mind.

He pictured to himself a man whom he had never seen; a tall, lean man with shoulders slightly stooped and a face seamed by rough weather and hard living more than with the years he had lived. The man was, Gary guessed, in his late forties. His eyes were a keen blue, his mouth thin-lipped and firm. Gary felt that if he removed the stained gray hat he wore, he would reveal a small bald spot on the crown of his head. Over one eye was a jagged scar. Another puckered the skin on his left cheek bone. He was dressed in gray flannel shirt and khaki overalls tucked into high, laced boots.

Gary visualized him as being the man who had built this cabin. He thought that he was picturing Waddell, and it occurred to him that Waddell might have been mining a little in Johnnywater Cañon. The man he was mentally visualizing seemed to be of the type of miner who goes prospecting through the desert. And Johnnywater Cañon certainly held mineral possibilities, if one were to judge by the rock formation and the general look of the cañon walls.

Gary himself had once known something about minerals, his dad having sent him to take a course in mineralogy at Denver with a view to making of his son a respectable mining engineer. Gary had spent two years in the school and almost two years doing field work for practice, and had shown a certain aptitude for the profession. But Mills, the motion-picture director, had taken a company into Arizona where Gary was making a report on the minerals of a certain district, and Gary had been weaned away from mines. Now, he was so saturated in studio ideals and atmosphere that he had almost forgotten he had ever owned another ambition than to become a star with a company of his own.

Well, this man then—the man about whom he found himself thinking so intently—must have found something here in the cañon. He did not know why he believed it, but he began to think that Waddell had found gold; though it was not, properly speaking, a gold country. But Gary remembered to have noticed a few pieces of porphyry float on the bluff the morning that he had spent in looking for the man who shouted in the night. The float might easily be gold-bearing. Gary had not examined it, since he had been absorbed in another matter. It is only the novice who becomes excited and builds air castles over a piece of float.

Gary turned his head abruptly and looked back, exactly as he would have done had a man approached and stood at his shoulder. He was conscious of a slight feeling of surprise that the man of whom he was thinking did not stand there beside him.

"I'll be getting 'em too, if I don't look out," he snorted, and dumped the mottled cat unceremoniously on the floor.

It has been said by many that thoughts are things. Certainly Gary's thoughts that evening seemed live things. While he was washing the dishes and sweeping the cabin floor, he more than once glanced up, expecting to see the man who looked like a miner. The picture he had conjured seemed a living personality, unseen, unheard, but nevertheless present there in the cabin.

Gary was an essentially practical young man, not much given to fanciful imaginings. He did not believe in anything to which one may permissibly attach the word psychic. Imagination of a sort he had possessed since he was a youngster, and stories he could weave with more or less originality. He did not, therefore, run amuck in a maze of futile conjecturing. He believed in hunches, and there his belief stopped short, satisfied to omit explanations.

That night fell pitch black, with inky clouds pushing out over the rim rock and a wind from the west that bellowed across the cañon and whipped the branches of the pines near the cabin. Above the clouds played the lightning, the glare of it seeping through between the folds and darting across small open spaces.

Gary sat in the doorway watching the clouds with the lightning darting through. True to his type and later training, he was thinking what a wonderful storm scene it would make in a picture. And then, without warning, he heard a voice shouting a loud halloo from the bluff. Again it called, and ended with a wail of pain.

Gary started. He turned his face to the cañon side and listened, deep lines between his eyebrows. It was almost a week since he had heard the call, and it did not seem natural that the man should be shouting again from the same point on the bluff. He had been so sure that the fellow, whoever he was, had left the cañon that first night. It was absolutely illogical that he should return without coming near the cabin.

Gary got up and stood irresolute in the doorway. The voice was insistent, calling again and again a summons difficult to resist.

"Hel*lo-oo-ooh*! Hel*lo-oo-ooh*!" called the voice.

Gary cupped his hands around his mouth to reply, then hesitated and dropped them to his side. He turned to go in for the lantern and abandoned that idea also. On that first night he had answered repeatedly the call and had searched gropingly amongst the bowlders and ledges. His trouble had gone for nothing, and Gary could think of but one reason why he had failed to find the man: he believed the man had not wanted to be found, although there was no sense in that either. The stubborn streak in Gary dominated his actions now. He meant to find the fellow and have it out with him. He remembered Monty's remark about Waddell imagining he heard things, and selling out in a hurry, his nerves gone to pieces. Probably the man up on the bluff could explain why Waddell left Johnnywater!

Gary crossed the creek during spurts of lightning, and made his way cautiously up the bluff. After spending a long forenoon there he knew his way fairly well and could negotiate ledges that had stopped him that first night. He went carefully, making himself as inconspicuous as possible. The voice kept shouting, with now and then a high note that almost amounted to a shriek.

The storm broke, and Gary was drenched to the skin within five minutes. Flashes of lightning blinded him. He stumbled back down the bluff and reached the cabin, the storm beating upon him furiously. As he closed the door, the voice on the bluff shrieked at him, and Gary thought there was a mocking note in the call.

CHAPTER NINE
GARY WRITES A LETTER

"Johnnywater Cañon.

"Dear Pat:

"I take it all back. There's a new model of cow called Walking X, that don't need grass. It has a special food-saving device somewhere in its anatomy, which enables it to subsist on mountain scenery, sagebrush and hopes. I haven't discovered yet whether the late model of Walking X chews a cud or merely rolls a rock under its tongue to prevent thirst. I'm guessing it's the rock. There's darned little material for cuds in the country. If I were going to stay here and make you a cattle queen, I should ask you to get prices on gum in carload lots.

"Yesterday I was hiking out on the desert—for exercise, my dear girl. Can't afford to grow flabby muscled as well as flabby souled. Souls don't register on the screen anyway—but it takes muscle to throw the big heavy around in the blood-curdling scrap which occurs usually in the fourth reel. Besides, I'm going to throw a fellow down the bluff—when I get him located. Don't know how big he is, as I haven't met the gentleman yet. It's a cinch he hasn't got lung trouble though; he's the longest-winded cuss I ever heard holler.

"He's been trying to get fresh with me ever since I came. Picks wild, stormy nights when a man wants to stay indoors and then gets up on the bluff and hollers for help. First couple of nights I heard him, I bit. But I don't fall for that hokum any more. A man that can holler the way he does and come back strong the next night don't need any assistance from me.

"I hoed your spuds to-day, Pat. Did a perfect imitation of Charlie Ray—except that I wasn't costumed for the part. Didn't have no gallus to hitch up and thereby register disgust with my job. But I featured the sweat—a close-up of me would have looked like Gary out in a rain. It was accidental. I was chasing Pat Connolly's pigs, trying to round them up and get acquainted. They headed for Pat Connolly's alfalfa and they went through the potato patch. There ought to be a fence around those spuds, Pat; or else the pigs ought to be shut up. You're a darn shiftless ranch lady to let pigs run loose to root up your spuds. They're in full blossom—and don't ask me which I mean, pigs or potatoes. They needed a little strong-arm work, bad. The pigs ducked out of the scene into the alfalfa—and that sure needs cutting, too. There's a scythe in the shed, and a fork or two and a hay rake. If Waddell's got horses he couldn't have used them much. Maybe he couldn't afford a mowing machine, and cut his hay with a scythe. There's a wagon here, and a comedy hayrack. But I can't feature handsome Gary scything hay.

"Anyway, every darned spud blossom in the patch peeked up at me through a jungle of weeds. That wouldn't look good to a buyer (you won't get a chance to read this letter, old girl, so I don't mind telling you you've played right into my hands with that Power of Attorney, and I'm going to sell out, if Monty Girard ever comes and hauls me back to town). They're not finished yet, but I can do the rest in the morning if Monty don't come.

"Monty Girard has plumb forgotten me, I guess. He was a friendly cuss, too. He's seven days overdue, and I'd get out and hunt him up, only he forgot to leave me his address and I can't get his 'phone number from Information. Can't get Information. There ain't no telephone. He said his camp was about twenty miles off. But I'm wise to these desert miles. More likely it's thirty. I tried to trail him yesterday, but he took our back track for five miles or so, and for all I know he may have beat it back to town. That's not walking distance, I'll tell a heartless world.

"I'm stuck here until somebody comes and hauls me away. The last house I saw was back down the road a nice little jaunt of about sixty-five miles. Monty Girard drives his Ford like he was working in one of those comedy chases. And it's four hours by the watch from that last shack to this shack—Monty Girard driving. Figure it yourself, Pat, and guess how many afternoon calls I've made on my neighbors. I'm afraid the pinto cat couldn't walk that far, and it would hurt her feelings if I didn't ask her to join the party.

"Said pinto cat is a psychic. Waddell was a nut of some kind, and the cat caught it. Seems Waddell got the habit of seeing things—though I haven't located any still yet—and now the cat looks up and meows at the air, and rubs her fur against her imagination. Got my goat the first time she did it—I admit it. I can't say I feature it yet, her talking and playing up to some gink I can't see. But I named her Faith and I've no kick coming, I reckon, if the eyes of Faith looks up to things of which I kennest not.

"I'm wondering if Waddell wasn't a tall, round-shouldered gink with a bald spot on top of his head the size of a dollar and a half, and a puckered scar on his cheek; a Bret Harte type, before he puts on the mustache. I keep thinking about a guy like that, as if he belonged here. When Faith takes one of her psychic fits, I get a funny idea she's trying to rub up against that kind of a man. Sounds nutty, but heck knows I never did feature the spook stuff, and I don't mean I'm goofy now about it. I just keep thinking about that fellow, and there's times when I get a funny notion he's standing behind me and I'll see him if I look around. But get this—it's good. *I don't look around!* It's over the hills to the bug-house when a fellow starts that boob play.

"There's something wrong about this trick cañon, anyway. I can't seem to feature it. You can't make me believe that boob up on the bluff thinks he's a cuckoo clock and just pops out and hollers because he's made that way. He's trying to get my goat and make me iris out of the scene. There's going to be a real punch in the next reel, and that guy with the big voice will be in front of it. His head is swelled now since he's scared Waddell out. But he's going to get a close-up of yours truly—and the big punch of the story.

"The other night just after dark I sneaked up the bluff as high as I could get without making a noise so he'd hear me, and laid for him. I was all set to cut loose with that blood-curdling Apache yell dad's riders used to practice when I was a kid. But he never opened his mouth all night. Made a fool out of me, all right, losing my sleep like that for nothing. Then the next night he started in at sundown and hollered half the night.

"I'm overdue at the studio now, by several days. If Mills could get that contract for me, it's gone blooey by this time. And he can't get word to me or hear from me—I'm not even famous enough yet to make good publicity out of my disappearance. Soon as Monty comes, I intend to beat it in to Las Vegas and wire Mills. Then if there's nothing doing for me in pictures right now, I'll get out and see how good I am as a salesman.

"But I hate to let that four-flusher up here in the rocks think he's got the laugh on me. And that alfalfa ought to be put up, and no mistake. The spuds need water, too. After the trusty hoe has got in its deadly work on the weeds, a good soaking would make them look like a million dollars. And I suppose the pigs ought to be shut up before they root up all the spuds on the place— but then some one would have to be here to look after them. That's the heck of it, Pat. When you get a place on your hands, you simply let yourself in for a dog's life, looking after it.

"You had a picture of me riding out at dawn after the cattle! That shows how much you don't know. All told there's about fifteen head of stock that water here at the mouth of the creek. I mean, at the end of the creek where it flows into a big hole and forgets to flow out again. It acts kind of tired, anyway, getting that far; no pep to go farther. As for horses, Monty and I looked for your horses as we came across the desert out here. There wasn't a hoof in sight, and Monty says they're probably watering over at another spring about fifteen miles from here. It's too far to walk and drag a loop, Pat. So your dashing Western hee-ro can't dash. Nothing to dash on. That's a heck of a note, ain't it?

"Did you ever try to make three meals fill up a day? Well, don't. Can't be did. I've read all the magazines—the whole two. I also have read Mr. Waddell's complete library. One is 'Cattle and Their Diseases,' and the other is 'Tom Brown's School Days,' with ten pages gone just when I was getting a kick out of it. That was one day when it rained. I knew a man once who could go to bed at sundown and sleep till noon the next day. I don't believe he kept a psychic cat, though, or chased voices all over the hills. Anyway, I forgot to find out how he did it.

"This looks a good cañon for mineral. Something tells me some rich stuff has been taken out of here. If I were going to stay any length of time, I might look around some. I keep thinking about gold—but I guess it's just a notion. Monty Girard ought to be here to-morrow, sure. I've packed my pyjamas every morning and unpacked them every night. I've got as much faith as the pinto cat—but it don't get me a darn bit more than it gets her. Packing my pyjamas and waiting for Monty Girard is just about as satisfactory as the cat's rubbing up against nothing. You'd think she'd get fed up on that sort of thing, but she don't. Just before I started to write, she trotted toward the door looking up and purring like she does when I come in. Only nobody came in. You wouldn't notice it if there was anybody else around. Being alone makes it creepy.

"I started this because I wanted to talk to somebody. Being alone gets a fellow's goat in time. And seeing I don't intend to send this to you, Pat, I'll say I'm crazy about you. There's not another girl in the world I'd want. I love the way you stand by your own ideas, Pat, and use your own brains. If you only knew how high you stack up alongside most of the girls, you wouldn't worry about who played opposite me. I was sore when I left you that night—but that was just because I hate to see you lose your money, and that 'flabby-soul' wallop put me down for the count.

"I'll admit now that you didn't get cheated as much as I thought; but I'm here to remark also that Johnnywater Cañon is no place for my Princess Pat to live. And it's a cinch that Handsome Gary is not going to waste his splendid youth in this hide-out. There goes that darned nut on the bluff again, yelling hello at me.

"If Monty Girard doesn't show up to-morrow I'm sure as heck going to figure out some way of getting at that bird. Yesterday he was hollering in the daytime. He's crazy, or he's trying to make a nut out of me. I believe he wants this cañon to himself for some reason, and tries to scare everybody out. But I don't happen to scare quite as easy as Waddell. Though the joke of it is, I couldn't get out of here till Monty Girard comes, no matter how scared I got. I'm sure glad I never get sick.

"Golly grandma, how I hate that howling! I'd rather have coyotes ringed around the cañon four deep than listen to that merry roundelay of the gink on the bluff. I'd take a shot at him if I had a gun.

"Good night, Pat. You're five hundred miles away, but if every inch was a mile I wouldn't feel any farther or any lonesomer. Your flabby-souled movie man is going to bed.

"Gary."

CHAPTER TEN
GARY HAS SPEECH WITH HUMAN BEINGS

Since Gary was not a young man of pronounced literary leanings, he failed to chronicle all of the moods and the trivial incidents which borrowed importance from the paucity of larger events. He finished hoeing the potatoes and spent a mildly interested half-day in running the water down the long rows, as Waddell's primitive system of irrigation permitted.

That evening there was no voice shouting from the hillside, and Gary spent a somberly ruminative hour in cleaning the mud off his shoes. He was worried about his clothes, which were looking the worse for his activities; until it occurred to him that he had passed and repassed a very efficient-looking store devoted to men's clothing alone. It comforted him considerably to reflect that he could buy whatever he needed in Las Vegas.

On the eleventh day he started down the cañon on the chance that he might see Monty coming across the desert. The tall piñon trees shut out the view of the open country beyond until he came almost abreast of the last pool of the creek where the cattle watered. He was worrying a good deal now over Monty Girard. He could not believe that he had been deliberately left afoot there in the cañon, as effectively imprisoned as if four stone walls shut him in, held within the limit of his own endurance in walking. Should he push that endurance beyond the limit, he would die very miserably.

Gary was not particularly alarmed over that phase of his desertion, however. He knew that he was not going to be foolish enough to start out afoot in the hope of getting somewhere. Only panic would drive a man to that extreme, and Gary was not of the panicky type. He had food enough to last for a long time. The air, as he told himself sardonically, was good enough for any health resort. He didn't feel as if he could get sick there if he tried. His physical well-being, therefore, was not threatened; but he owned himself willing to tell a heartless world that he was most ungodly lonesome.

He was walking down the rough trail with his hands in his pockets, whistling a doleful ditty, the spotted cat at his heels like a dog. He was trying to persuade himself that this was about the time of day when Monty would be most likely to show up, when Faith ran before him, stopped abruptly, arched her back and ruffled her tail at something by the water hole.

Gary stopped also and stared suspiciously at two men who were filling canteens at the water hole. What roused Gary's suspicion was the manner of the two men. While they sunk their canteens beneath the surface of the water and held them so, they kept looking up the cañon and at the bluff across the creek; sending furtive, frightened glances into the piñon grove.

"Hello!" shouted Gary, going toward them. The cañon wall echoed the shout. The two dropped their canteens and fled incontinently out toward the open. Gary walked over to the pool, caught the two canteen straps, filled the canteens and went after the men, considerably puzzled. He came upon them at their camp, beside a ten-foot ledge outcropping, a hundred yards or so below the pool. They were standing by their horses, evidently debating the question of moving on.

"Here's your canteens," Gary announced as he walked up to them. "What's the big idea—running off like that?"

"Hello," one responded guardedly. "We don't see who hollers. That's bad place. Don't like 'm."

They were Indians, though by their look they might almost be Mexicans. They were dressed much as Monty Girard had been clothed, in blue overalls and denim jacket, with old gray Stetson hats and coarse, sand-rusted shoes.

Gary lowered the canteens to the ground beside their little camp fire and got out his tobacco and papers, while he looked the two over.

"So you think it's a bad place, do you? Is that why you camp out here?"

"Them cañon no good," stated the other Indian, speaking for the first time. "Too much holler all time no see 'm. That's bad luck."

"You mean the man up on the bluff, that hollers so much?" Gary eyed them interestedly. "Who is he? You fellows know anything about it?"

They looked at one another and muttered some Indian words. The old man began to unpack the apathetic mule standing with dropped lip behind the two saddle horses.

"You know Monty Girard?" Gary asked, lighting his cigarette and proffering his smoking material to the younger Indian when he saw an oblique glance go hungrily to the smoke.

"Yass! Monty Girard. His camp by Kawich," the old man answered in a tone of relief that the subject had changed.

"Well, I don't know where Kawich is—I'm a stranger in the country. Seen him lately?" Gary waved his hand for the younger Indian to pass the tobacco and papers to the older buck. "Seen Monty lately?"

"Nah. We don't see him, two months, maybe." The old buck was trying to conceal his pleasure over the tobacco.

Gary thought of something. "You see any Walking X horses—work horses, or saddle horses?"

With characteristic Indian deliberation the two waited until their cigarettes were going before either replied. Then the old man, taking his time in the telling, informed Gary that the horses were ranging about ten miles to the east of Johnnywater, and that they were watering at a small spring called Deer Lick. It occurred to Gary that he might be able to hire these Indians to run in the horses so that he could have a saddle horse at least and be less at the mercy of chance. With a horse he could get out of the country without Monty and the Ford, if worst came to worst.

He squatted with the Indians in the shade of the ledge while they waited for the water to boil in a bent galvanized bucket blackened with the smoke of many camp fires, and set himself seriously to the business of winning their confidence. They were out of tobacco, and Gary had plenty, which helped the business along amazingly. He caught himself wishing they wore the traditional garb of the redman, which would have been picturesque and satisfying. But these Piutes were merely unkempt and not at all interesting, except that their speech was clipped to absolutely essential words. They were stodgy and apathetic, except toward the tobacco. He found that they could dicker harder than a white man.

They wanted ten dollars for driving in his horses, and even then they made it plain to Gary that the price did not include getting them into the corral. For ten dollars they would bring the horses right there to the mouth of the cañon.

"Not go in," the old man stipulated. "Bring 'm here, this place. Not corral. No. No more. You take my horse, drive 'm to corral. I wait here."

Gary knew a little about Indians, and at the moment he did not ask for a reason. The corral was not a quarter of a mile farther on; as a matter of fact it was just beyond the cabin at the edge of the grove of piñons.

Faith came out from a clutter of rocks and hopped into Gary's arms, purring and rubbing herself against him. The Piutes eyed the cat askance.

"B'long 'm Steve Carson, them cat," the young Indian stated abruptly. "You ain't scare them cat bad luck?"

Gary laughed. "No—I'm not afraid of the cat. Faith and I get along pretty well. Belongs to a Steve Carson, you say? I thought this was Waddell's cat. It was left here when Waddell sold out."

They deliberated upon this, as was their way. "Waddell sell this place?" The old Indian turned his head and looked into the cañon. "Hunh. You buy 'm?"

"No. A friend of mine bought it. I came here to see if it's any good." Gary began to feel as if he were making some headway at last.

They smoked stolidly.

"No good." The old man carefully rubbed the ash from his cigarette. "Bad spirits. You call 'm bad luck." He looked at Gary searchingly. "You hear 'm holler?"

Gary grinned. "Somebody hollers about half the time. Who is it?"

The two looked at each other queerly. It was the younger one who spoke.

"Them's ghos'. When Steve go, comes holler. Nobody holler when Steve's all right. Five year them ghos' holler. Same time Steve go. Nobody ketchum Steve. Nobody stop holler."

"Well, that's a heck of a note!" Gary smoothed the cat's back mechanically and tried to laugh. "So the Voice is Steve Carson's ghost, you think? And what happened to Steve?"

"Dunno. Don' nobody know. Steve, he makes them shack. Got cattle, got horses, got chickens. Mine a little, mebby. One time my brother she go there. No ketchum Steve Carson no place. Hears all time holler up there. My brother holler. Thinks that's Steve, mebby. My brother wait damn long time. Steve don't come. All time them holler up on hill. My brother thinks Steve's hurt, mebby. My brother goes. Hunts damn long time. Looks all over. No ketchum Steve. My brother scare, you bet!

"My brother comes my place. Tells Steve Carson, he's hurt, hollers all time. Tells no ketchum Steve no place. I go, my father goes. Other mans go. Hunt damn long time. Nobody hollers. No ketchum Steve Carson. Saddle in shed, wagon by tree, canteens hang up, beans on stove—burnt like hell. Them cat holler all time.

"By 'm by we go. Hunt two days, then go. We get on horses, then comes holler like hell up on hill. Get off horses. Hunt some more. All night. No ketchum holler. No ketchum Steve no place. Them cat go 'Yeouw! Yeouw!' all time like hell.

"My brother, she's damn 'fraid for ghos'. My brother gets on horse and goes away from that place. Pretty soon my brother dies. That's five years we don't find Steve Carson. All them time holler comes sometimes. This place bad luck. Injuns don't come here no more, you bet. We come here now little while when sun shines. Comes night time it's damn bad place. You hear them hollers you don't get scared?" It would seem that Gary's assertion had not quite convinced them. The young Indian was plainly skeptical. According to the judgment of his tribe, it was scarcely decent for a man to foregather with ghosts and feel no fear.

The mottled cat squirmed out of Gary's embrace and went bounding away among the rocks. The eyes of the Indians followed it inscrutably. The old man got up, clawed in his pack, pulled out a dirty cloth in which something was tied. He opened the small bundle, scooped a handful of tea and emptied it into the bucket of boiling water. The young man opened a savage-looking pocket knife and began cutting thick slices of salt pork. The old Indian brought a dirty frying pan to the fire.

Gary leaned against the rock ledge and watched them interestedly. After so long an exile from all human intercourse, even two grimy Piutes meant much to him in the way of companionship. They talked little while they were preparing the meal. And when they ate, squatting on their heels and spearing pork from the frying pan with the points of their big jackknives, and folding the pieces around fragments of hard, untempting bannock, they said nothing at all. Gary decided that eating was a serious business with them and was not to be interrupted by anything so trivial as conversation.

He wanted to hear more about the Johnnywater ghost and about Steve Carson. But the Piutes evidently considered the subject closed, and he could get nothing more out of them. He suspected that he had his sack of Bull Durham to thank for the unusual loquacity while they smoked.

After they had eaten they led their horses up to the pool and let them drink their fill. After that they mounted and rode away, in spite of Gary's urging them to camp where they were until they had brought in the Walking X horses. They would go back, they said, to Deer Lick and camp there for the night. In the morning they would round up his horses and drive them over to Johnnywater.

Gary was not quite satisfied with the arrangement, but they had logic on their side so far as getting the horses was concerned. Their own mounts would be fresh in the morning for the work they had to do. But the thing Gary hated most was their flat refusal to spend a night at Johnnywater Cañon.

CHAPTER ELEVEN
"HOW WILL YOU TAKE YOUR MILLIONS?"

"Johnnywater Cañon,

"On a Dark and Gloomy Night.

"My Princess Pat:

"You are the possessor of a possession of which you wittest not. You have a ghost. Wire Conan Doyle, Sir Oliver Lodge and others of their ilk. Ask them what is the best recipe for catching a Voice. The gink up on the bluff that does so much vocal practice is not a gink—he's a spook. He's up there vocaling right now, doing his spookish heckest to give me the willies.

"Pat, did you send me out here just from curiosity, to see if I'd go goofy? Tut, tut! This is no place for a flabby-souled young man; broad shoulders, my dear girl, don't amount to a darn in grappling with a man-size Voice. I believe you did, you little huzzy. I remember you distinctly mentioned howling on a hill, and my sitting in the cabin listening to it. Great idea you had. I'm sitting here listening. What am I supposed to do next?

"You also indicated business of listening to a horse champing hay in a stable. Well, I have a horse at last, but the property man overlooked the sod-roofed stable. Not having the prop in which my horse should champ, he's picketed up the cañon, and he's supposed to be champing sagebrush or grass or something. He isn't doing it though. He absolutely refuses to follow direction. He's up there going 'MMMH-*hmmm-Hmmm*-hm-hm-hm!!!!' I'm sorry, Pat, but that's exactly what he's doing—as close as it can be put into human spelling. He can't feature this cañon, honey. I suspect he's flabby souled, too.

"He wants to chase off with the rest of the bunch about ten or fifteen miles. Nobody loves this cañon except the psychic cat and the two pigs. And the pigs don't love it any more; not since I made a rock corral and waylaid the little devils when they went snooping in there after some stuff I put in a trough. I baited the trap, you see—oh, this gigantic brain of mine has been hitting on all two cylinders lately!—and then I hid. Lizards crawled over me, and the sun blistered the back of my neck while I waited for those two brutes to walk into the foreground. Animal pictures are hard to get, as you may have heard while you were enduring a spasm of Handsome Gary's shop talk. Cut. Iris in Gary sneaking up with the board gate he'd artcrafted the day before. So the pigs don't love Handsome Gary any more, and they're spending most of their spare time talking about me behind my back and hunting for a soft place where they can run a drift under my perfectly nice rock fence, and then

- 45 -

stope up to the surface and beat it, registering contempt. I'll call 'em shoats if they don't behave.

"I scythed some alfalfa to-day, Pat. Put on a swell rural comedy, featuring Handsome Gary making side-swipes at his heels. It was a scream, I reckon. But I came within an inch of scything Faith, only she's a wizard at jumping over rocks and things, and she did as pretty a side-slip as you ever saw, and made her get-away. I've wondered since—would I have had two pinto cats, or only one psychic Voice? I mean one more psychic Voice. This one up on the bluff used to belong to Steve Carson, according to the yarn the Piutes told me. He'd have made a great director, if the rest of him measured up to his lung power. The Piutes say he faded out very mysteriously, five years ago, leaving his holler behind him. I'm afraid folks didn't like him very well. At any rate his Voice is darned unpopular. I can't say it makes any great hit with me, either. Though it's not so bad, at that. The main trouble seems to be not having any man to go with the Voice. The Piutes couldn't feature it at all. They wouldn't drive the horses into the corral, even. I had to double for them when they got the bunch down there at the mouth of the cañon. Jazzed around for two hours on an Injun pony with a gait like a pile driver, getting your horses into your corral. You seem to have four or five fair imitations, Pat. The rest are the bunk, if you ask me. Not broken and not worth breaking. Don't even look good to eat.

"There is one work team which I mean to give a try-out when I put on my character part entitled, Making Hay Whether the Sun Shines or Not. They have collar marks, and they're old enough to be my dad's wedding team. Lips hang down like a mule, and hollows over their eyes you could drop an egg in. I hate to flatter you, kid, but your horse herd, take it by and large, is not what I'd be proud of. You're a wonderful girl—you got stung in several places at once.

"Haven't seen anything yet of Monty Girard. Can't think what's the matter, unless that savage Ford of his attacked him when he wasn't looking. It will be just as well now if he holds off till I get your alfalfa cut and stacked. I'll have a merry heck of a time doing it alone. There's about four acres, I should judge. To-morrow morning I start in and do a one-step around the patch with that cussed scythe. You needn't think it's going to be funny—not for Handsome Gary. I tried to get the youngest Piute to double for me in the part, but nothing doing. 'Them holler no good,' is what he said. Funny—I kinda feel that way myself. Money wouldn't tempt 'em. He spoke well of Steve Carson, too; but he sure as heck don't like his voice.

"What would you say, kid, if I found you a mine in here? I've had the strongest hunch—I can't explain it. I keep thinking there's a mine up on the bluff where that Voice is. I suppose I can trace the idea back to that porphyry float I picked up the day after I landed here. I found another piece yesterday, lying out here behind the cabin. It must have been packed in from somewhere else. Pretty rich-looking rock, kid. If I could find enough of that, you wouldn't need to pound out invoices and gol-darned letters about horse feed and what to wean calves on. You could have a white mansion topping that hill of ours, where we climb up and sit under the oak while we build our air castles. Will we ever again? You feel farther away than the sun, kid. I have to write just to keep my thoughts from growing numb with the damned chill of this place. You know—I wrote it down before. It's hell to be wondering what you'd see if you looked around....

"Well, if I find you a mine you can have your mansion on the hill. Because, if the mine stacked up like the rock I found, you could carry a million dollars around with you careless-like for spending money—street-car fare, you know, and a meal at the cafeteria, and such luxuries. And if your pocket was picked or your purse snatched or anything, you could wave your hand airily and say, 'Oh, that's all right. I've hundreds of millions more at home!' How'd you like that, old girl?

"Because I mortared a piece of that rock and panned it. It was rich, Pat—so darned rich it scared me for a minute. I thought I had a bad case of Desert Rat's Delusion. I wouldn't tell you this, kid, if I ever meant to send the letter. I'm just writing to please myself, not you. No, sir, I wouldn't tell you a word about it. I'd just go ahead and open up the mine—after I'd found it—and get about a million dollars on the dump before I let a yip out of me. Then maybe I'd send you word through your lawyer saying 'I begged to inform you that I had dug you a million dollars, and how would you have it?' Golly grandma, if I could only find the ledge that rock came from!

"You know, Pat, you got me all wrong that night. What made me so doggoned sore was to think how you'd handed over five thousand dollars to a gink, just on the strength of his say-so. It showed on the face of it that it was no investment for you to make. It wasn't that I am so stuck on the movies. Heck knows I'm not. But I sure am stuck on the job that will pay me the money I can get from working in the movies. I'll rent my profile any time—for a hundred dollars a day, and as much more as I can get. That's what the contract would have paid me the first year, Pat, and double that the second if I made good. So I was dead willing to put paint on my eyebrows and paint on my lips, and let my profile—if you insist that's all I got over on the screen—earn a little home for my Princess Pat and me.

"But if I could find a mine to match that chunk of rock, the studios would never see Handsome Gary—never no more. I'd kiss my own girl on the lips—for love. Honest, Pat, those kisses, that looked so real on the screen and made you so sore, were awfully faked. I never told you. I guess I'm a mean cuss. But I never touched a girl's lips, Lady, after I met you. I had one alibi guaranteed never to slip. I told 'em, one and all, confidentially before we went into the scene, that they could trust me. I swore I'd remember and not smear their lips all over their cheeks. I said I knew girls hated that, and I'd be careful. Then it was up to me to do some plain and fancy faking. And when my Lady Patricia put up her chin and registered supreme indifference, it always tickled me to see how well I'd put it over. I always meant to tell you some time, girlie.

"I had a wild idea when I left the city that I'd maybe write down a story I'd been framing in my mind when I was on location and waiting between scenes. I told Mills just enough of it to get him curious to hear the rest. He told me to write it out in scenario form and if it was good he'd see that the company bought it. That would have been a couple of hundred more toward our home, kid. The point is, I laid in a lot of paper. Now that darn story's gone stale on me and I'm using up the paper writing letters to you that you'll never read. As a little blond jane in our company was always saying, 'Isn't life a perfect *scream*?' I'll say it is.

"Your Grouchy Gary."

CHAPTER TWELVE
MONTY APPEARS

Monty Girard, mounted on a lean-flanked sorrel, came jogging up the trail into Johnnywater Cañon. His eyes, that managed to see everything within their range of vision, roved questingly here and there through the grove, seeking some sign of the fastidiously tailored young man he had left there two weeks before. His horse went single-footing up to the cabin and stopped when Monty lifted his rein hand as a signal.

"Hello!" Monty shouted buoyantly, for all he had just finished a twenty-mile ride through desert heat. He waited a minute, got no reply, and dismounted.

He pushed open the door and went in, his eyes betraying a shade of anxiety. The cabin was clean, blankets spread smoothly on the bunk. He lifted a square of unbleached cloth that had once been a flour sack which covered sugar, salt, pepper, condensed milk and four tin teaspoons, lately scoured until they almost shone, leaning bowls up in an empty milk can. Also a white enameled bowl two thirds full of dried apples and raisins stewed together. Monty heaved a sigh of relief. The movie star was evidently keeping house just like a human.

Monty went out and stood at the corner of the cabin near the horse. There was nothing the matter with his lungs, but the rest of him was tired. He hunted Gary by the simplest means at his command. That is, he cupped his palms around his mouth, curved his spine inward, planted his feet rather far apart, and sent a loud "Hello!" echoing through the cañon.

The thin-flanked sorrel threw up its head violently and backed, stepped on the dragging reins and was brought up short. Monty turned, picked up the reins and drawled a reproof before he called again. Four times he shouted and proceeded then to unsaddle. If the movie star were anywhere within Johnnywater Cañon he could not fail to know that he had a caller come to see him.

Five minutes later Monty glanced up and stared with his mouth slightly open. Gary was sneaking around the corner of the cabin with raised pitchfork in his hands and a glitter in his eyes. When he saw who it was, Gary lowered the pitchfork and grinned sheepishly.

"When you holler hello in this cañon, *smile!*" he paraphrased whimsically, and drew his shirt sleeve across his forehead. "Thought I'd landed that trick Voice at last. Well, darn it, how are you?"

"All right," Monty grinned slowly, "if you just put down that hay fork. What's the matter? You gittin' like Waddell?"

Gary leaned the pitchfork against the cabin. He pushed his hair back from his forehead with a gesture familiar to audiences the country over.

"By heck, I hope not," he exclaimed brusquely. "I'd given up looking for you, Monty. And that cussed Voice sounded to me like it had slipped. I've got used to it up on the hill, but I sure as heck will take a fall out of it if it comes hollering around my humble hang-out. Where's the Ford?"

Monty pulled saddle and blanket together from the back of the sorrel, leaving the wet imprint shining in the sun. The sorrel twitched its hide as the air struck through the moisture coldly.

"Well, now, the old Ford's done been cremated ever since the night I left here," Monty informed him pensively. "Yuh-all recollect we had quite a wind from the west that night. Anyway, it blowed hard over to my camp. I started a fire and never thought a word about the Ford being on the lee side of camp, so first I knew the whole top of the car was afire. I just had time to give her a start down the hill away from camp before the gas tank blowed up. So that left me afoot, except for a saddle horse or two. Then I had some ridin' to do off over the other way. And I knew yuh had grub enough to last a month or two, so I didn't hurry right over like I would have done if yuh-all needed anything." His keen eyes dwelt upon Gary's face with unobtrusive attention.

The young movie star, he thought, had changed noticeably. He was a shade browner, a shade thinner, more than a shade less immaculate. Monty observed that he was wearing a pair of Waddell's old trousers, tucked into a pair of Waddell's high-laced boots with the heels worn down to half their height, the result of climbing over rocks. Gary's shirt was open with a deep V turned in at the collar, disclosing a neck which certain sentimental extra girls at the studio had likened to that of a Greek god. Gary's sleeves were rolled up to his elbows. He looked, in short, exactly as any upstanding city chap looks when he is having the time of his life in the country, wearing old clothes—the older, the better suited to his mood—and roughing it exuberantly.

Yet there was a difference. Exuberant young fellows from the city seldom have just that look in the eyes, or those lines at the corners of the mouth. Monty unconsciously adopted a faintly solicitous tone.

"How yuh-all been making it, anyway?" he asked, watching Gary roll a cigarette.

"Finest ever!" Gary declared cheerfully, lighting a match with his thumb nail, a trick he had learned from an old range man because it lent an effective touch sometimes to his acting.

"A couple of Piutes happened along the other day, and I had them run in the horses for me. Thought I'd keep up a saddle horse so I could round up a team of work horses when I get ready to haul the hay." He blew a mouthful of smoke and gave a short laugh. "I'm a heck of a stock hand for a gink that was born on a horse ranch." He blew another mouthful of smoke deliberately, not at all conscious that he was making what is termed a dramatic pause, nor that he was making it with good effect. "I owe Pat Connolly," he said slowly, "a cheap saddle horse. I'm glad Pat hadn't learned to love that scrawny bay. Where can I get a horse for about a dollar and six bits?"

Monty eyed him dubiously. "Yuh-all mean yuh lost a hawse?"

"No-o, I didn't exactly *lose* a horse. It died." Gary sat down in the doorway and folded his arms upon his knees.

"I ought to have had more sense," he sighed, "than to stake him out so close to the shed where the sack of grain was. I sort of knew that rolled barley is not good as an exclusive diet for horses. I had a heck of a job," he added complainingly, "digging a hole big enough to plant him in."

Monty swore sympathetically; and after the manner of men the world over, related sundry misfortunes of his own by way of giving comfort. Gary listened, made profane ejaculations in the proper places, and otherwise deported himself agreeably. But when Monty ceased speaking while he attended to the serious business of searching his most inaccessible pockets for a match, Gary broached a subject altogether foreign to Monty's plaintive reminiscences.

"Say, Monty! Was Waddell tall and kind of stoop-shouldered and bald under his hat? And did he have blue eyes and a kind of sandy complexion and lips rather thin—but pleasant, you know; and did he always wear an old gray Stetson and khaki pants tucked into boots like these?"

Monty found the match, in his shirt pocket after all. A shadow flicked across his face. Perhaps even Monty Girard had an instinct for dramatic pauses and hated to see one fall flat.

"Naw. Waddell wasn't a very tall man and he was dark complected; the sallow kind of dark. His eyes was dark, too." He examined the match rather carefully, as if he were in some doubt as to its proper use. He decided to light it and lifted a foot deliberately, so that he might draw the match sharply across the sole.

"That description of yours," he said, flipping the match stub away from him and watching to see just where it landed, "tallies up with Steve Carson. Yuh ain't——" He turned his head and regarded curiously the Gary Marshall profile, which at that moment was absolutely impassive. "It was Steve cut the logs and built this cabin," he finished lamely.

Gary unfolded his arms and stretched his legs out straight before him. "What happened to this Steve Carson?" he asked innocently. "Did he sell out to Waddell?"

Monty smoked absent-mindedly, one spurred heel digging a little trench in the dirt.

"That's Steve's cat," he observed irrelevantly, glancing up as Faith came out of the bushes, picking her way carefully amongst the small rocks that littered the dooryard.

"Uh-huh." Gary drew up his legs and clasped his hands around his knees. "If this Steve Carson didn't sell out to Waddell, then where does Waddell come into the scene? Did Steve Carson give the darned thing away?"

Monty leaned forward, inspecting the small trench his spur had dug. Very carefully he began to rake the dirt back into it.

"It ain't gettin' yuh, is it?" He did not look up when he asked the question. He was painstakingly patting the dirt smooth with the toe of his boot.

"*Getting* me! Hell!" said Gary.

"It got Waddell—bad," drawled Monty, biting a corner of his lip. "That's why he sold out. It was gettin' him. Bad." Having filled the trench and patted the dirt smooth, Monty straightway began to dig another trench beside it.

"What is there to get a fellow?" Gary looked challengingly at Monty. "I've stayed with it two weeks, and I haven't been got yet." He laughed a little. "The Piutes told me a man disappeared here and left his Voice behind him. Of course that's Injun talk. What's the straight of it, Monty?"

"Well—nobody ever called me superstitious yet," Monty grinned, "but that's about the size of it. Steve Carson came up missing. Since then, there's that Voice. I know it started in right away. I was over here helping hunt for him, and I heard it. Some says Steve went loco and tried to walk out. If he did, he left mighty unexpected, and he didn't take anything at all with him. Not even a canteen, far as I could see. He had two, I know—and they was both hangin' on the same nail beside the door. Uh course, he might a had another one— I hadn't been over to Johnnywater for a coupla months, till I come over to see what was wrong. I was scoutin' around the country for a week or more, tryin' to get some trace of him."

Having completed the second trench, Monty filled that one as carefully as he had filled the first. Abruptly he looked at Gary. "Yuh-all ain't—*seen* anything, have yuh?"

CHAPTER THIRTEEN
"I DON'T BELIEVE IN SPOOKS"

A silence significant, almost sinister, fell. Gary rose from the doorsill, took a restless step or two and turned, so that he faced Monty, and the open doorway. He looked past Monty, into the cabin. A quick glance, almost a furtive one. Then he laughed, meeting Monty's inquiring eyes mockingly.

"Seen anything? No. Nothing I shouldn't see, at least. Why?" He laughed again, a mirthless kind of laugh. "Did Waddell throw in a spook along with the Voice?"

"Waddy got powerful oneasy," Monty observed, choosing his words with some care. "Waddy claimed he seen Steve Carson frequent. I didn't know——Say! Did the Piutes tell yuh-all how Steve Carson looked?"

Gary's eyes slid away from Monty's searching look.

"No. I didn't ask. I just got a notion that Waddell maybe looked like that." He lifted his chin, his glance once more passing Monty by to go questing within the cabin.

"I don't believe in spooks," he stated clearly, a defiant note creeping into his voice in spite of him. "That's the bunk. When people start seeing spooks, it's time they saw a doctor and had their heads X-rayed. I'll tell you what I think, Monty. I think that when we check out, we stay *out*. Get me? I can't feature giving death all these encores—when, damn it, the audience is sitting hunched down into its chairs with its hands over its faces, afraid to look. If we clapped and stamped and whistled to get 'em out before the curtain, then I'd say they had some excuse.

"I tell you, Monty, I've got a lot of respect for the way this Life picture is being directed. And it don't stand to reason that a director who's on to his job is going to let a character that was killed off in the first reel come slipping back into the film in the fourth reel. I know what *that* would mean at Cohen's. It would mean that some one in the cutting room would get the gate. No, sir, that's bad technique—and the Big Director up there won't stand for any cutbacks that don't help the story along." His eyes left Monty's face to send another involuntary glance through the open door. "So all this hokum about ghosts is pure rot to me."

"Well, I ain't superstitious none myself," Monty repeated somewhat defensively. "I never seen anything—but one time I was here when Waddy thought *he* seen something. He tried to point it out to me. But I couldn't see nothin'. I reckon you're right. And I'm shore glad yuh-all feel that way."

The spotted cat, having dined well upon a kangaroo rat caught down by the creek, was sitting near them calmly washing her face. She got up, looked up into the open doorway, and mewed a greeting. Then she trotted to meet—a memory, perhaps. She stopped three feet from the doorstep and stood there purring, her body arched with a rubbing movement.

Monty Girard turned his head and stared at the cat over his shoulder. Three deep creases formed between Gary's eyebrows while he also watched the pantomime. The cat turned, looked up ingratiatingly (still, perhaps, clinging to a memory) and trotted away toward the creek exactly as if she were following some one. Monty got up and the eyes of the two men met unsmilingly.

"Oh, heck," said Gary, shrugging his shoulders. "Come on and see the hay I've put up!"

They walked in a constrained silence to the alfalfa field. Monty cast a critical eye over the raggedy edge of the cutting. He grinned slowly, tilting his head sidewise.

"Whereabouts did yuh-all learn to swing a scythe?" he asked banteringly. "I reckon yuh could do it a heap better on a hawse."

"But the darned horse idea blew up on me. Did the balloon stunt. You get me, don't you?" Gary's laugh hinted at overstrained nerves. "I wish you'd been here then, Monty. Why, I didn't dig any grave. I had to excavate a cellar to plant him in." He waved a hand toward the haycocks. "How do you like the decorations? You will observe that they are somewhat larger than were being worn by meadows last year. These are the new 1921 models, specially designed with the stream-line effect, with a view to shedding rain. Also hail, snow and any other form of moisture. They are particularly good where horses are unavailable for hauling hay to a stack."

"I'll run in the horses to-morrow," Monty volunteered casually. "The two of us together ought to get that hay hauled in a day, all right. Spuds is lookin' good. I reckon this ain't your first attempt at farming."

"The first and the last—I'll tell a waiting world. Say, I forgot you might be hungry. If this new hay won't give your horse acute gastritis, why not tie him down by the cabin and carry him a forkful or two? I can't feature this corral stuck off here by itself where we can't keep an eye on it. Still, if you say it's all right, we'll put him in."

Monty said it was all right, and Gary did not argue. His spirits had reacted to the stimulus of Monty's presence, and he was conscious now and then of a heady feeling, as if he had been drinking champagne. His laughter was a bit too frequent, a shade too loud to be perfectly normal. The mental pendulum, having been tilted too far in one direction, was swinging quite as far the other way in an effort to adjust itself to normalcy.

Monty Girard was not of an analytical temperament, though circumstance had forced him to observe keenly as a matter of self-protection. He apprehended Gary's mood sufficiently to let him set the tempo of their talk. Gary, he remembered, had been two weeks alone in Johnnywater Cañon. By his own account he was wholly unaccustomed to isolation of any degree. Monty, therefore, accepted Gary's talkative mood as a perfectly natural desire to make up for lost time.

But there was a reserve in Gary's talk, nevertheless, an invisible boundary which he would not pass and which held Monty Girard within certain well-defined conversational limits. It seemed to pass directly through Gary's life at Johnnywater, and to shut off completely the things which Monty wanted most to know. Of all the trivial, surface incidents of those two weeks, Gary talked profusely. His amusing efforts to corral the pigs and keep them there; his corraling of the horses on the old Piute's hard-gaited pony; his rural activities with hoe and irrigating shovel; all these things he described in great detail. But of his mental life in the cañon he would not speak.

But Monty Girard was observing, and he watched Gary rather closely during the three days which he spent at Johnnywater. He saw Gary's lips tighten when, on the second evening just after supper, the Voice shouted unexpectedly from high up on the bluff. He saw a certain look creep into Gary's eyes, and the three little creases show themselves suddenly between his eyebrows. But the next moment Gary was looking at Monty and laughing as though he had not heard the Voice.

Monty Girard, having eyes that saw nearly everything that came within their range of vision, saw also this: He saw Gary frequently rise, walk across the cabin and stand with his back leaning against the wall, facing the place where he had been sitting. He would continue his laughing monologue, perhaps— but his eyes would glance now and then with reluctance toward that place, as if he were testing an impression. After a bit of that, Gary would return and sit down again, resuming his old careless manner. The strange, combative look would leave his eyes and his forehead would smooth itself.

Gary never spoke of these things, and Monty Girard respected his silence. But he felt that, although he knew just what the pigs had done and how long it took to corral the horses and how many blisters it took to "scythe" the hay, he would remain in ignorance of Gary's real life in Johnnywater Cañon, the life that was changing him imperceptibly but nevertheless as surely as old age creeps upon a man who has passed the peak of his activities.

"Yuh-all better ride on over with me to my camp and stop there till you get a chance to ride in to town," Monty said, when they were unhooking the team from the hay wagon after hauling in the last load of alfalfa. "Yuh can turn the pigs loose again and let 'em take their chances on the coyotes, same as they was doin' when yuh come. Some one's liable to come drivin' in to my camp any day. But," he added significantly, "yuh'll set a long time before anybody comes to Johnnywater."

"That's all right," Gary said easily, pulling the harness off the horse he was attending to, and beginning to unbuckle the collar strap, stiff and unruly from disuse. "I'll just stick here for awhile, anyway. Er—the potatoes need a lot of man-with-the-hoe business." His fingers tugged at the collar strap. He would not look up from his work, though he knew that Monty was eyeing him steadily over the sweaty backs of the horses.

"I'd kill that damned cat if I was you," Monty exploded with a venom altogether foreign to his natural manner. "Waddy'd never let it near the house. He never did and I never knowed why till the other day."

Gary had one expression which usually silenced all argument. Patricia called it his stubborn smile. Dead men who have gone out fighting sometimes wear that same little smile frozen immutably upon their features. It was that smile which answered Monty Girard.

Monty looked at him again, puzzled and more than slightly uneasy.

"Yuh better come along with me," he said again, persuasively, as one urges the sick to follow the doctor's orders.

"No—I think I'll just stick around for awhile." Having removed the collar, Gary gave the horse a slap on the shoulder that sent it off seeking a soft spot on which to roll.

"Well, for God's sake, kill that cat! By gosh, it's enough to drive a fellow crazy. It's wrong in the head and—and yuh know it might have hydrophoby."

Gary laughed. "Why, I couldn't keep house without the pinto cat! That's great business. Furnishes atmosphere and—er—entertainment."

It was perfectly apparent that Gary had some secret reason for staying. Something which he would not tell Monty Girard, although the two had become rather good friends. Monty's face clouded; but Gary slapped him reassuringly on the shoulder.

"Tell you what you do, old fellow. You draw me a map so I can find my way over to your place later on. And if one of these horses is any good under the saddle, I'll keep him in the corral so I'll have something to ride. Now I've got hay, the beggar ought to make out all right."

Monty had to be content with that and rode away to his own camp somewhat reluctantly, leaving Gary standing in the doorway of the cabin, his hands braced against the frame on either side, smoking and staring after him a bit wistfully.

CHAPTER FOURTEEN
PATRICIA REGISTERS FURY

Patricia waited a week. One day at the office when she happened to be alone for half an hour, she jerked the telephone hook off its shelf and looked up Cohen's studio number. Inwardly she was furious. She would be a long time forgiving Gary for forcing her to speak the first word. She could see no possible excuse for such behavior, and her voice, when she spoke into the mouthpiece, was coldly impersonal.

"Will you please tell me where I can get into touch with Mr. Mills' company?" Patricia might have been calling up the freight office to put a tracer on a lost shipment of ground barley.

"Mr. Mills' company is out on location," replied a voice which Patricia mentally dubbed snippy.

"I asked you where I could get in touch with Mr. Mills' company. This is important." Patricia spoke into a dead telephone. The snippy one in Cohen's office had hung up.

While Patricia was still furious, she wrote a note to Gary. And, since her chin had squared itself and her head ached and she hated her job and the laundry had lost the collar to her favorite vestee, Patricia's note read like this:

"Los Angeles, Calif.

"June 17, 1921.

"Gary Herbert Marshall,
"Cohen's Studio,
"Hollywood, Calif.

"Dear Sir:

"Kindly return the papers which you carried off with you a week ago last night.

"Very truly,

"P. Connolly."

Patricia mailed this letter along with a dozen invoices, fourteen "please remits" and a letter to the main office in Kansas City. She felt better after she had poked it into the mail box. She could even contemplate buying a new vestee set without calling the laundry names.

Patricia waited a week and then called Cohen's studio again. She was quite prepared for another snub, and perhaps that is the reason why she got it. Mr.

Mills' company was on location; and Patricia could believe that or not, just as she chose. Patricia did not believe it. She barked a request for Mr. Gary Marshall.

"We do not deliver telephone messages to actors," the snippy one informed Patricia superciliously, and hung up before Patricia could enunciate the scathing retort she had ready.

That night at seven o'clock Patricia called Gary's apartment. Her mood was such, when she dialed the number, that a repair man had to come the next day and replace a broken spring in the instrument. She held the receiver to her ear a full five minutes and listened to the steady drone of the bell calling Gary. Had Gary been there to answer, he would have had a broken engagement within five minutes to hold him awake nights.

After awhile little Pat Connolly wiped the tears of rage from her eyes and called the landlady of Gary's apartment.

The landlady assured her that Mr. Marshall hadn't been near the place for two weeks. At least, she had not seen him. He might have come in late and gone out early—a good many of her tenants did—and in that case she wouldn't be so apt to see him. But she hadn't noticed him around last Sunday, and most generally she did see him Sundays because he slept late and if she didn't see him she was pretty sure to hear his voice in the hall speaking to some one. She could always tell Mr. Marshall's voice as far as she could hear it, it was so pleasant——

"Oh, my good heavens!" gritted Patricia and followed the example of the snippy office girl at Cohen's. She hung up while the landlady was still talking. Which was not polite of Patricia, but excusable.

Well, perhaps Gary was out on location. But that seemed strange, because even after quarrels Gary had never failed to call Patricia up and let her know that he was leaving town. After quarrels his voice would be very cool and dignified, it is true; but nevertheless he had never before failed to let her know that he was leaving town.

Patricia spent another week in mentally reviewing that last evening with Gary and in justifying herself for everything she had said to him. Gary really did need to be told the plain truth, and she had told him. If he wanted to go away and nurse his injured vanity and sulk, that merely proved how much he had needed the plain truth told him.

She waited until Friday morning. On Friday, because she had not heard from Gary, and because she had lain awake Thursday night telling herself that she was thankful she had found him out in time, and that it didn't make a particle of difference to her whether she ever heard from him or not, Patricia manufactured an errand down town for her employers. Because she was a conscientious young woman she attended to the manufactured errand first. Immediately thereafter she marched into the branch office of the *Examiner*.

In years Patricia's chin had never looked so square. She was not in the habit of wetting her pencil, but now she stood at the ad counter, licked an indelible pencil defiantly, and wrote this, so emphatically that the pad was marked with the imprint of the letters seven pages deep:

> WANTED: Man to take charge of small cattle ranch in Nevada. Open range, living springs, imp. Completely furnished on shares. Phone 11270 Sun.

Patricia read this over twice with her lips buttoned in tightly. Then she licked the pencil again—indelibly marking her pink tongue for an inch down the middle—and inserted just before the 'phone number, the word "*permanent*" and drew two lines underneath for emphasis. This was meant as a trenchant warning to Gary Marshall that he need not trouble himself any further concerning Patricia's investment nor about Patricia herself, for that matter.

Patricia paid the display ad rate and marched out, feeling as irrevocably committed to cynical maidenhood as if she had taken the veil. Men as such were weak, vain creatures who thought to hold the heart of a woman in the curve of an eyelash. Meaning, needless to say, Gary Marshall's eyelash which should *not* longer hold the heart of Patricia Connolly.

Patricia's telephone began ringing at six o'clock on Sunday morning and continued ringing spasmodically until ten minutes past twelve, when Patricia dropped the receiver off the hook and let it dangle, thereby giving the busy signal whenever 11270 was dialed.

For six hours and ten minutes Patricia had felt a definite sinking sensation in her chest when a strange voice came to her over the 'phone. She would have wanted to murder any one who so much as hinted that she hoped to hear Gary say expostulatingly, "For heck's sake, Pat, what's the big idea of this ad? I can't *feature* it!"

Had she heard that, Patricia would have gloried in telling him, with the voice that went with the square chin, that she was sorry, but the place was already taken. Then she would have hung up and waited until he recovered from that wallop and called again. Then—well, Patricia had not decided definitely just what she would do, except that she was still firmly resolved upon being an old maid.

At seven o'clock in the morning the first man called to see her. Patricia was ready for him, clothed in her office tailored suit and her office manner. The man's name was Hawkins, and he seemed much surprised to find that a young woman owned the "small cattle ranch in Nevada."

Hawkins informed Patricia, in the very beginning of their conversation, that he was a fair man who never yet had cheated any one out of a nickel. He said that if anything he was too honest, and that this was the reason why he hadn't a ranch of his own and was not independent. He said that he invariably let the other fellow have the big end of a bargain, rather than have the load on his conscience that he had possibly not been perfectly square. As to cheating a woman, well, he hinted darkly that killing was too good for any man who would take advantage of a woman in a business deal. Hawkins was so homely that Patricia knew he must be honest as he said he was. She believed practically everything he said, and by eight o'clock on a calm Sunday morning, P. Connolly and James Blaine Hawkins were partners in the ranch at Johnnywater.

James Blaine Hawkins was so anxious that Patricia should have practically all the profits in the deal, that he dictated terms which he facetiously urged her never to tell on him; they were so one-sided (Patricia's side). Hawkins, in his altruistic extravagance, had volunteered to devote his time, labor and long experience in cattle raising, to almost the sole benefit of Patricia. He was to receive merely two thirds of the increase in stock, plus his living expenses. For good measure he proposed to donate the use of his car, charging Patricia only for the gas and oil.

Patricia typed the agreement on her machine, using all the business phrases she had learned from taking dictation in the office. The document when finished was a beautiful piece of work, absolutely letter perfect and profusely decorated with whereases, be it therefore agreeds and—of course—hereofs, party of the first parts and party of the second parts. Any lawyer would have gasped over the reading. But James Blaine Hawkins considered it a marvelous piece of work and said so. And Patricia was mightily pleased with herself and drew a sigh of relief when James Blaine Hawkins had departed with a signed copy of the Patricia-made AGREEMENT OF CONTRACT in his pocket. Patricia held the original; held it literally for the next two hours. She read it over and over and couldn't see where one word could be changed for the betterment of the document.

"And what's the use of haggling and talking and whittling sticks over a simple thing like this?" Patricia asked a critical world. "Mr. Hawkins knew what he wanted to do, and I knew what I wanted to do—and talking for a week wouldn't have accomplished anything at all. And anyway, that's settled, and I've got Johnnywater off my mind for the next five years, thank Heaven. Gary Marshall can go on smirking the rest of his life if he wants to. I'm sure it's absolutely immaterial to me."

Gary Marshall was so absolutely immaterial to Patricia that she couldn't sleep nights, but lay awake telling herself about his absolute immateriality. She was so pleased over her agreement with James Blaine Hawkins that her boss twice stopped his dictation to ask her if she were sick or in trouble. On both occasions Patricia's glance turned him red in the face. And her "Certainly not" gave the poor man a guilty feeling that he must have insulted her somehow.

Patricia formed a habit of walking very fast from the car line to Rose Court and of having the key to her mail box in her fingers when she turned in from the street. But she absolutely did not want or expect to receive a letter from Gary Marshall.

Curiously, Cohen's telephone number kept running through her mind when her mind had every reason to be fully occupied with her work. She even wrote "Hollywood 741" when she meant to write "Hollister, Calif." on a letter she was transcribing. The curious feature of this freak of her memory is that Patricia could not remember firm telephones that she used nearly every day, but was obliged to keep a private list at her elbow for reference.

Patricia did not call Hollywood 741. She did, however, write a second stern request for her papers which Gary had taken away.

On the heels of that, Patricia's boss—a kindly man in gold-bowed spectacles and close-cropped whiskers—gave Patricia a terrific shock when she had taken the last letter of the morning's correspondence and was slipping the rubber band over her notebook.

"Oh, by the way, Miss Connolly, day after to-morrow I leave for Kansas City. I'm to have charge of the purchasing department there, and I should like to have you with me if you care to make the change. The salary will be twenty-five a month more—to start; if the work justifies it, I think you could safely look forward to another advance. And of course your traveling expenses will be met by the firm."

Patricia twisted her pencil in the rubber band. "My laundry won't be back till Friday," she informed him primly. "But I suppose I can go out there and pay for it and have it sent on by mail. What train are you taking, Mr. Wilson?"

In this manner did the dauntless Patricia meet the shock of opportunity's door slamming open unexpectedly in her face. Patricia did not know that she would like Kansas City. She had a vague impression of heat and cyclones whenever she thought of the place. But it seemed to her a Heaven-sent chance to show Gary Marshall just how immaterial he was in her life.

She debated the wisdom of sending back Gary's ring. But the debate did not seem to get much of anywhere. She left for Kansas City with the ring still on her finger and the hope in her heart that Gary would be worried when he found she was gone, and would try to find her, and would fail.

And Providence, she told herself confidently, had surely been looking after her all along and had sent James Blaine Hawkins to take that darned Johnnywater white elephant off her hands just nicely in time for the boss to offer her this change. And she didn't care how much she hated Kansas City. She couldn't hate it half as much as she hated Los Angeles.

It merely illustrates Patricia's firmness with herself that she did not add her reason for hating Los Angeles. In May she had loved it better than any other place on earth.

CHAPTER FIFTEEN
"WHAT'S THE MATTER WITH THIS PLACE?"

With his beautifully typed AGREEMENT OF CONTRACT in his inner coat pocket, and two hundred dollars of Patricia's money in his purse, James Blaine Hawkins set out from Los Angeles to drive overland to Johnnywater, Nevada. He knew no more of Johnnywater than Patricia had told him, but he had worked through three haying seasons on a big cattle ranch in King County, California, and he felt qualified to fulfill his share of the agreement, especially that clause concerning two thirds of the increase of the stock and other profits from the ranch.

James Blaine Hawkins belonged to that class of men which is tired of working for wages. A certain percentage of that class is apparently tired of working for anything; James Blaine Hawkins formed a part of that percentage. His idea of raising range cattle was the popular one of sitting in the shade and watching the cattle grow. In all sincerity he agreed with Patricia that one simply *cannot* lose money in cattle.

I am going to say right here that James Blaine Hawkins owned many of the instincts for villainy. He actually sat in Patricia's trustful presence and wondered just how far the law protected an absent owner of squatter's rights on a piece of unsurveyed land. He thought he would look it up. He believed that the man who lives on the place is the real squatter, and that Waddell, in leaving Johnnywater, had legally abandoned the place and had no right to sell his claim on it to Patricia or any one else.

James Blaine Hawkins did not look Patricia in the eyes and actually plan to rob her of Johnnywater, but he did sit there and wonder who would have the best title to the place, if he went and lived there for a year or two, and Patricia failed to live there at all. To James Blaine Hawkins it seemed but common justice that the man who lived on a ranch so isolated, and braved the hardships of the wilderness, should acquire unqualified title to the land. He did not discuss this point, however, with Patricia.

Patricia's two hundred dollars had been easily obtained as an advance for supplies, which, under the terms of the contract, Patricia was to furnish. So James Blaine Hawkins was almost enthusiastic over the proposition and couldn't see why three or four years at the most shouldn't put him on Easy Street, which is rainbow's end for all men of his type.

He made the trip without mishap to Las Vegas, and was fortunate enough to find there a man who could—and did—give him explicit directions for reaching Johnnywater. And along about four o'clock on the afternoon of the fourth day, Patricia's new partner let down a new wire gate in the mended fence across the cañon just above the water hole, and gazed about him with an air of possession before he got into the car and drove on to the cabin. He did not know, of course, that the gate was very new indeed, or that the fence had been mended less than a week before. He was therefore considerably astonished when a young man with his sleeves rolled to his elbows and the wind blowing through his hair came walking out of the grove to meet him.

James Blaine Hawkins frowned. He felt so much the master of Johnnywater that he resented the sight of a trespasser who looked so much at home as did Gary Marshall. He grunted a gruff hello in response to Gary's greeting, drove on into the dooryard and killed his engine.

Gary turned back and came close to the car. He was rather quick at reading a man's mood from little, indefinable signs which would have been overlooked by another man. Something in the general attitude of James Blaine Hawkins spelled insolence which Gary instinctively challenged.

"Are you lost?" Gary asked rather noncommittally. "You're pretty well off the beaten track, you know. This trail ends right here."

"Well, that suits me. Right here is where I headed for. Might I ask what you're doing here?"

"Why, I suppose you might." Now that Gary had taken a good look at James Blaine Hawkins, he did not like him at all.

James Blaine Hawkins waited a reasonable time for Gary to say what he was doing in Johnnywater Cañon. But Gary did not say. He was rolling a cigarette with maddening precision and a nonchalant manner that was in itself an affront; or so James Blaine Hawkins chose to consider it.

"Well, damn it, what *are* you doing here?" he blurted arrogantly. James Blaine Hawkins was of the physical type which is frequently called beefy. His red face darkened and seemed to swell.

"I? Why, I'm stopping here," drawled Gary. "What are *you* doing here?"

James Blaine Hawkins leaned against the side of the car, folded his arms and spat into the dust. Then he laughed.

"I'm here to stay!" he announced somewhat pompously. "I don't reckon it's any of your business, but I've got a half interest in this place—better 'n a half interest. I got what you might call a straight two thirds interest in everything. Two thirds and *found.*" He laughed again. "So, I guess mebby I got a right to know why you're stopping here."

Not for nothing was Gary Marshall an actor. When he learned to portray emotion before the camera, he also learned to conceal emotion. Not even

Patricia in her most suspicious mood could have discovered how astonished, how utterly taken aback Gary was at that moment.

He lighted his cigarette, blew out the match and flipped it from him. He took three long, luxurious inhalations and studied James Blaine Hawkins more carefully from under the deep-fringed eyelashes that had helped to earn him a living. Patricia, he perceived, had been attacked by another "wonderful" idea. Though it seemed rather incredible that even the impulsive Patricia should have failed to read aright a man so true to type as was James Blaine Hawkins.

"Well, I've saved you a few tons of alfalfa hay," Gary observed carelessly. "Fellow I was with left me here while he went on to another camp. I found Waddell gone, and my friend hasn't come after me yet. So I'm stuck here for the present, you see. And Waddy's hay needed cutting, so I cut it for him. Had to kill time somehow till he gets back." Gary blew a leisurely mouthful of smoke. "Isn't Waddell coming back?" he asked with exactly the right degree of concern in voice and manner.

James Blaine Hawkins studied that question for a minute. But he could see nothing to doubt or criticize in the elucidation, so he decided to accept it at face value. He failed to see that Gary's explanation had been merely suggested.

"Waddell, as you call him, has sold out to a girl in Los Angeles," James Blaine Hawkins explained in a more friendly tone. "I got an agreement here to run the place on shares. I don't know nothing about Waddell. He's out of it."

Gary's eyebrows lifted slightly in what the camera would record as his terribly worried expression.

"He isn't—in the—er—asylum, is he? Was I too late to save poor Waddy?"

James Blaine Hawkins looked blank.

"Save him from what? What yuh talkin' about, anyway?"

Gary opened his lips to answer, then closed them and shook his head. When he really did speak it was quite plain to James Blaine Hawkins that he had reconsidered, and was not saying as much as he had at first intended to say.

"If you're here to stay, I hope you'll be all right and don't have the same thing happen to you that happened to Waddy," he said cautiously. "I think, myself, that Waddell had too keen an imagination. He was a nervous cuss, anyway; I really don't think you'll be bothered."

"Bothered with what?" James Blaine Hawkins demanded impatiently. "I can't see what you're driving at."

Gary gave him a little, secretive smile and the slight head-shake that always went with it on the screen.

"Well, I sure hope you never do—see." And with that he deliberately changed the subject and refused artfully to be led back toward it.

He went in and started the fire going, saying that he knew a man couldn't drive out from Las Vegas without being mighty hungry when he arrived. He made fresh coffee, warmed over his pot of Mexican beans cooked with chili peppers, and opened a can of blackberry jam for the occasion. He apologized for his biscuits, which needed no apology whatever. He went down to the creek and brought up the butter, bewailing the fact that there was so little of it. But then, as he took pains to explain again, he had not expected to stay so long when he arrived.

James Blaine Hawkins warmed perceptibly under the good-natured service he was getting. It was pleasant to have some one cook his supper for him after that long drive across the desert and it was satisfying to his vanity to be able to talk largely of his plans for running Johnnywater ranch at a profit. By the time he had mopped up his third helping of jam with his fourth hot biscuit, James Blaine Hawkins felt at peace with the world and with Gary Marshall, who was a fine young man and a good cook.

"Didn't make such a bad deal with that girl," he boasted, leaning back against the dish cupboard and heaving a sigh of repletion. "Kinda had a white elephant on her hands, I guess. Had this place here and nobody to look after it. Yes, sir, time I'd talked with her awhile, she was ready to agree to every damned thing I said. Got my own terms, ab-so-lute-ly. Five years' contract, and two thirds the increase of stock—cattle *and* horses—two thirds of all the crops—and *found!*"

"Get out!" exclaimed Gary, and grinned when he said it. "I suppose there *are* such snaps in the world, but I never saw one. She agreed to that? *On paper?*"

"On paper!" James Blaine Hawkins affirmed solemnly. He reached into his coat pocket (exactly as Gary had meant that he should). "Read it yourself," he invited triumphantly. "Guess that spells Easy Street in less than five years. Don't it?"

"It's a bird," Gary assured him heartily. Then his face clouded. He sat with his head slightly bowed, drumming with his fingers on the table, in frowning meditation.

"What's wrong?" James Blaine Hawkins looked at him anxiously. "Anything wrong with that contract?"

Gary started and with a noticeable effort pulled himself out of his mood. He laughed constrainedly.

"The contract? Why, the contract's all right—fine. I was just wondering——" He shook his shoulders impatiently. "But you'll be all right, I guess. A man of your type——" He forced another laugh. "Of course it's all right!"

"You got something on your mind," James Blaine Hawkins challenged uneasily. "What is it? You needn't be afraid to tell *me*."

But Gary forced a laugh and declared that he had nothing at all on his mind. And by his very manner and tone James Blaine Hawkins knew that he was lying.

The mottled cat hopped upon the doorstep, hesitated when she saw James Blaine Hawkins sitting there, then walked in demurely.

"Funny-looking cat," James Blaine Hawkins commented carelessly.

Gary looked up at him surprisedly; saw the direction of his glance, and turned and looked that way with a blank expression of astonishment.

"Cat? What cat?"

"*That* cat! Hell, can't you see that *cat*?" James Blaine Hawkins leaned forward excitedly.

Gary's glance wandered over the cabin floor. Toward Faith, over Faith and beyond Faith. He might have been a blind man for all the expression there was in his eyes. He turned and eyed James Blaine Hawkins curiously.

"You mean to say you—you see a *cat*?" he asked solicitously.

"Ain't there a cat?" James Blaine Hawkins half rose from his seat and pointed a shaking finger. "Mean to tell me that ain't a cat walkin' over there to the bunk?"

Gary looked toward the bunk, but it was perfectly apparent that he saw nothing.

"Waddell used to see—a cat," he murmured regretfully. "There used to be a cat that belonged to a man named Steve Carson, that built this cabin and used to live here. Steve disappeared very mysteriously awhile back. Five years or so ago. Ever since then——" He broke off suddenly. "Really, Mr. Hawkins, maybe I hadn't better be telling you this. I didn't think a man of your type would be bothered——"

"What about it?" A sallow streak had appeared around the mouth and nostrils of James Blaine Hawkins. "Yuh needn't be afraid to go on and tell me. If that ain't a cat——"

"There *was* a cat, a few years back," Gary corrected himself gently. "There was the cat's master, too. Now—they say there's a Voice—away up on the bluff, that calls and calls. Waddell—poor old duffer! He used to see Steve Carson—and the cat. It was, as you say, a funny-looking cat. White, I believe, with black spots and yellowish-brown spots. And half of its face was said to be white, with a blue eye in that side."

Gary leaned forward, his arms folded on the table. His voice dropped almost to a whisper.

"Is that the kind of a cat you see?" he asked.

James Blaine Hawkins got up from the bench as if some extraneous force were pulling him up. His jaw sagged. His eyes had in them a glassy look which Gary recognized at once as stark terror. A cold feeling went crimpling up Gary's spine to his scalp.

James Blaine Hawkins was staring, not at the cat lying curled up on the bunk, but at something midway between the bunk and the door.

Gary could see nothing. But he had a queer feeling that he knew what it was that James Blaine Hawkins saw. The eyes of the man followed something to the bunk. Gary saw the cat lift its head and look, heard it mew lazily, saw it rise, stretch itself and hop lightly down. He saw that terrified stare of James Blaine Hawkins follow something to the open doorway. The cat trotted out into the dusky warmth of the starlit night. It looked to Gary as if the cat were following some one—or some *thing*.

James Blaine Hawkins relaxed, drew a deep breath and looked at Gary.

"Did you see it?" he whispered, and licked his lips.

Gary shivered a little and shook his head. The three deep creases stood between his eyebrows, and his lips were pressed together so that the deep lines showed more distinctly beside his mouth.

"Didn't yuh—*honest?*" James Blaine Hawkins whispered again.

Again Gary shook his head. He got up and began clearing the table, his hands not quite steady. He lifted the dented teakettle, saw that it needed water and picked up the bucket. He hesitated for an instant on the doorstep before he started to the creek. He heard a scrape of feet behind him on the rough floor and looked back. James Blaine Hawkins was following him like a frightened child.

They returned to the cabin, and Gary washed the dishes and swept the floor. James Blaine Hawkins sat with his back against the wall and smoked one cigarette after another, his eyes roving here and there. They did not talk at all until Gary had finished his work and seated himself on the bunk to roll a cigarette.

"What's the matter with this damn place, anyway?" James Blaine Hawkins demanded abruptly in that tone of resentment with which a man tacitly acknowledges himself completely baffled.

Gary shrugged his shoulders expressively and lifted his eyebrows.

"What would you say was the matter with it?" he countered. "I know that one man disappeared here very mysteriously. An Indian, so they tell me, heard a Voice calling, up on the bluff. He died soon afterwards. And I know Waddell was in a fair way to go crazy from staying here alone. But as to what ails the place—one man's guess is as good as another man's." He lighted his cigarette. "I've quit guessing," he added grimly.

"You think the cabin's haunted?" James Blaine Hawkins asked him reluctantly.

Again Gary shrugged. "If the cabin's haunted, the whole darn cañon is in the same fix," he stated evenly. "You can't drag an Indian in here with a rope."

"It's all damn nonsense!" James Blaine Hawkins asserted blusteringly.

Gary made no reply, but smoked imperturbably, staring abstractedly at the floor.

"Wherever there's a spook there's a man at the back of it," declared James Blaine Hawkins, gathering courage from the continued calm. "That was a man I seen standin' by the bunk. Felt slippers, likely as not—so he wouldn't make no noise walkin'. He likely come in when I wasn't looking. And yuh needn't try to tell *me*," he added defiantly, "that wasn't no cat!"

Gary turned his head slowly and looked at James Blaine Hawkins.

"If there was a cat," he argued, "why the heck didn't I see it? There's nothing wrong with *my* eyes."

"I dunno why you never seen it," James Blaine Hawkins retorted pettishly. "*I* seen it, plain as I see you this minute. Funny you never seen it. I s'pose you'll say next yuh never seen that man standin' there by the bunk! He went outside, and the cat follered him."

Gary looked up quickly. "I didn't see any man," he said gravely. "There wasn't any man. I think you just imagined it. Waddell used to imagine the same thing. And he used to see a cat. He particularly hated the cat." James Blaine Hawkins gave a gasp. Gary looked at him sharply and saw that he was once more staring at the empty air near the door. The cat had come in again and was gazing questioningly about her as if trying to decide where she would curl herself down for a nap. The eyes of James Blaine Hawkins pulled themselves away from the terrifying vision near the door, and turned toward Faith. He gave a sudden yell and rushed out of the cabin.

Faith ran and jumped upon the bunk, her tail the size of a bologna sausage. Gary got up and followed James Blaine Hawkins as far as the door.

"Look out you don't hear the Voice, Mr. Hawkins," he said commiseratingly. "If I let my imagination get a fair running start, I couldn't stay in this cañon over night. I'd be a plain nut inside twenty-four hours."

James Blaine Hawkins was busy cranking his car. If he heard Gary speak he paid no attention. He got a sputter from the engine, rushed to the wheel and coaxed it with spark and gas-lever, straddled in over the side and went careening away down the trail to the open desert beyond.

Faith came inquisitively to the door, and Gary picked her up in his hands and held her, purring, against his face while he stroked her mottled back.

"I think you've saved little Pat Connolly a darned lot of trouble," he murmured into the cat's ear. "Thrashing that bird wouldn't have had half the effect."

CHAPTER SIXTEEN
"THERE'S MYSTERY HERE——"

"Dear Pat:—

"In God's name, what were you thinking of when you sent this fellow Hawkins over here with a five years' contract? Couldn't you see the man's a crook? Are the lawyers in Los Angeles all *dead*, that you couldn't call one up on the 'phone and ask a question or two about letting places on shares? Of course you'd want to write the contract yourself. Perfect Patricia is the little lady that invented brains! If she doesn't know all there is to know in the world, she'll go as far as she does know and fake the rest.

"Permit me to congratulate you, Miss Connolly, upon the artistic manner in which you handed over to James Blaine Hawkins the best imitation of a legacy that I ever saw! Of course you'd have to invent a new way of having your pocket picked. Two thirds and found! My word!

"Any ordinary, peanut-headed man would have given the usual one half of increase in stock, and the old stock made good at the end of the term of contract. And *not* found, Pat! No one but you would ever dream of doing a thing like that. And he says you agreed to buy his gas and oil. Pat, if ever a girl needed some one to look after her, you're that small person. And he bragged about it—the dirty whelp. Laughed at the way you met his terms and thought they were all right!

"He never came nearer a licking in his life and missed it, Pat. But I had another scheme, and I didn't want to gum it up by letting on I knew you. I had to sit pretty and let him brag, and register admiration for the rotter. He's gone now—it worked. But he'll come back—to-morrow, when the sun is shining and his blood thaws out again. I may have to lick him yet. If he were a white man, with the intelligence of a hen turkey, I could play the joker and make him lay down his hand. But I'll probably have to take a few falls out of him before I can convince him he's whipped from the start.

"You know, Pat, you've made an ungodly mess of things. In the whole sorry assortment of blunders you did just one thing that gives me a chance to save you. Before I left the city I made it a point to find out what kind of power runs a Power of Attorney, anyway. I happen to know a darned good lawyer, and I had a talk with him.

"Pat, you did something when you gave me that Power of Attorney. You gave me more right over the disposal of this place than if I were your husband. I came over here to use this right and sell Johnnywater. I think even James Blaine Hawkins will stop, look and listen when I tell him how come to-morrow.

"He'll come back. A good, strong dose of sunlight will bring him back—on the rampage, I'm guessing—mad to think how scared he was when he left. I played a dirty trick on him, Pat. I made him think the psychic cat was a spook.

"He thought it all right! But you see, I didn't know.

"I wonder if he really did see something. I think he did—or at any rate he kidded himself into thinking he did. I never dreamed he'd see.

"Pat, you called me flabby souled. That hurt—and it wasn't my vanity you hit. I've wanted you to respect me, Pat, in spite of my profession. And when you flung that at me, I saw you didn't understand. Lord knows I hate a whiner, and I won't try to explain just why I called you unjust.

"But after I got over here, Pat, I began to see the way I must have looked to you. You took at face value all the slams you've heard about the movies. You lumped us all together and called us cheap and weak and vain. Just puppets strutting around before the camera like damned peacocks. You couldn't see that maybe it takes quite as much character for a man to make good in the movies and live clean and honest, as it does to drive cows to water.

"But after all these hills and the desert out here beyond the cañon are mighty big and clean—my God, Pat, they'd shame the biggest man that ever lived! When you get out here and measure yourself alongside them you feel like a buffalo gnat on an elephant. And there's things in this cañon it takes a man to meet.

"There's mystery here; the kind you can't put your finger on. The kind the movies can't feature on the screen. Until James Blaine Hawkins drove into the scene, I'd have sworn a man could live here for forty years in the wilderness like the children of Israel—or maybe it was Noah and the ark—and never meet a villain who's out to make you either the goat or a corpse—both, maybe, if the story runs that way.

"But I've learned something I never knew before. I've learned there are things a man can fight that's worse than crooks. Dad was kind of religious, and he used to quote Bible at me. One of his favorite lines was about 'He that is master of himself is greater than he that taketh a city.' It sounded like the bunk to me when I was a kid. Now I kind of see what the old man was driving at. This country puts it right up to you, Pat.

"So, I'm going to find out something before I leave here, Pat. I want to know who's going to lick: Gary Marshall, or Johnnywater Cañon. It sort of dawned on me gradually that if I leave here now, I'll leave here licked. Licked by something that's never laid a finger on me! Scared out—like Waddell. Pat, my dear, I never could go back and face you if I had that to remember. Every time you looked at me I'd feel that you were calling me flabby souled in your heart—and I'd know I had it coming.

"Of course, I don't need to be hit with an axe in order to take a hint. I got the slap you sent me, Pat—along with James Blaine Hawkins. *You* know I'm over here. You know it as well as you know anything. Even if I didn't say I was coming—even though I *did* say I wasn't coming—you knew I came. You'd call up the studio, and Mills would tell you I was out of town on business. So you'd know; there's nothing else could take me out.

"So I got the slam you handed me, when you let the place to Hawkins for five years. You couldn't go into court, Pat, and swear that you didn't offer me the management of Johnnywater. The very fact that I have all the documents pertaining to the deal, plus the Power of Attorney, will prove that anywhere. Then Monty Girard knows it—a valuable witness, Monty. So I can save you from your own foolishness, and I'll do it, young lady, if I have to fight you in court. Hawkins is not going to get his two thirds and *found*! The two hundred he grafted off you I may not be able to save. But I'll keep the rest out of his clutches, make no mistake.

"I've got the glooms to-night, Pat. Feel sort of blue and sick at heart. It hit me pretty hard, reading that contract you drew up for Hawkins to brag about. It hurt to see him take that paper out of his pocket—paper that you had handled, Pat, words that you had typed. He's not fit to touch it. He left it here—lying on the table when he beat it, scared silly. You were stubborn when you signed your name—you did that to spite Gary. Own up now, Pat; didn't you do it just for spite—because I left without saying good-by? I wonder if it hurt you like it hurt me. I reckon not. Girls are so damned self-righteous—but then, they have the right. God knows, the best of men don't amount to much.

"There's something I want to do for you; if I don't do it before I leave here, it won't be for want of trying. You'll never make one dollar off this investment, just hanging on to it as it stands. This country's full of loco, for one thing. The percentage of loss is higher than my dad would ever have stood for. Practically every horse you own has got a touch of loco. And Monty says the calf crop is never up to normal. It's a losing game, in dollars and cents. A man could stay with it and make a bare living, I suppose. He could raise his own vegetables, put up enough hay to keep a horse or two, and manage to exist. But that would be the extent of it. And I don't want to see you lose—you won't, if I can help it. Having Hawkins in the deal may complicate matters—unless he quits. And, honey, I'll make the quitting as good as possible for him.

"I was sore when I started to write. But now I'm just sorry—and I love you, Pat. I wouldn't have you different if I could.

"Gary."

CHAPTER SEVENTEEN
JAMES BLAINE HAWKINS FINDS HIS COURAGE—AND LOSES IT

Gary had measured his man rather accurately, and his guess hit close to the mark. He slept late that morning, probably because he had lain awake until the morning star looked at him through the window. The sun was three hours high when he got up, and he loitered over his breakfast, gave Faith a severe talking to and fed her all the canned milk she would drink, so that she would not be teasing him for it later on when her insistence might be embarrassing. Faith was a methodical cat and a self-reliant cat. She loved her milk breakfast and her little talk with Gary afterward. Then she would head straight for the creek, cross it and go bounding away up the bluff. She always took the same direction, and Gary had sometimes wondered why. Of course, she hunted birds and kangaroo rats and mice; she was an expert huntress. Gary thought she must keep a private game preserve up on the bluff somewhere. However that might be, Faith was off for her daily prowl on the bluff and would not show up again at the cabin until noon or later.

Gary was up at the corral rubbing down the chunky little sorrel horse he called Jazz, when he heard the chug of a motor coming up-grade through the sand. James Blaine Hawkins, he knew without looking, had discounted his terror of last night and was returning to take possession.

"Well, Jazz, if I get the gate, there's your new master." Gary slapped the horsefly that was just settling on the sorrel's neck. "But I won't tell you good-by till I'm gone."

He turned and went down to the cabin, reaching it just as James Blaine Hawkins stopped in the dooryard. Gary chose to take the return as a matter of course.

"Had your breakfast, Mr. Hawkins?" Gary asked him genially. "The coffee may still be hot. I had a pretty good fire while I was washing the dishes. Thought I'd cook up a mess of beans. Takes a heck of a while to cook them in this altitude."

James Blaine Hawkins gave him a look that might easily be called suspicious. But Gary met it innocently.

"I've et," James Blaine Hawkins grunted. "Camped out on the desert—better than walking distance away from whoever it was that tried to get funny last night. Feller don't know what he's going up against, in a strange place like that after dark. But there can't nobody bamboozle me, once I've got my bearings!"

His whole manner was a challenge. He eyed Gary boldly, watching for some overt act of hostility. He climbed out of the car and began to unpack, with a great deal of fussing and mighty little accomplished.

Gary did not say anything. He leaned against the cabin with his arms folded and watched James Blaine Hawkins indifferently. His silence affected the other unpleasantly.

"Well, why don't you say something? What yuh standin' there grinnin' that way for? Why don't yuh own up you know a damn sight more'n what yuh let on?" he demanded pugnaciously.

James Blaine Hawkins came toward him, his fists opening and closing nervously at his side. "I ain't to be bluffed, you know! I ain't to be bluffed *nor* scared!"

Gary's lip curled. He rubbed the ash from his cigarette against a splinter on the log wall beside him.

"You're brighter than I thought," he drawled. "I *do* know a damn sight more than I'm saying. I'll say as much of what I know as I happen to choose. No more—and bullying won't get you anything at all. I might have told you a few things last night, if you hadn't got scared and beat it."

"Scared? Who was scared?" fleered James Blaine Hawkins. "Not me, anyway. I seen right away there was some kind of frame-up agin me here and I didn't want no trouble. Any fool can go head down into trouble, but a man uh brains'll side-step till he knows what he's up against."

"Well," smiled Gary, "do you know what you're up against?"

"Sure, I know! For some reason, somebody don't want me here. They tried to scare me last night—but I seen through that right off."

"Yes, you saw more than I did," Gary told him quietly.

"Well, and what's all this you know?" Hawkins' voice was rising angrily. "I'm here to stay. I want to know what's back of all this."

Gary took an exasperating time to reply. "If you find out, you'll do more than Waddell did," he said at last. His face was sober, his tone convincing. "I've a little matter of my own to discuss with you, but that has nothing whatever to do with last night. Last night you claimed to see a man—and there *wasn't* any man. You know darned well there wasn't, or you wouldn't have been so scared. That's something I have nothing to do with. I didn't see any one in the cabin—but you." He smoked for another minute. "You also claimed you saw a cat." He looked at James Blaine Hawkins steadily.

"I claimed to and I *did!* There's a frame-up of some kind. You said yourself——"

"I said Waddell thought *he* saw things here. That's the plain truth, Hawkins. It worried Waddell so he nearly went crazy, from all accounts. You needn't take my word for that. You can ask the Indians, or Monty Girard—any one who knows this place."

He stopped and drew some legal papers from his pocket. "Here's something I meant to show you last night—if you had stayed," he said. "I'm not in the habit of babbling my business to every chance stranger. I didn't tell you, because I wanted to make sure that it concerned you. But it happens that I have a prior right here. That's what brought me over here in the first place. It's true I wanted to see Waddell, and he was gone when I arrived. But I knew all about the sale, Mr. Hawkins. I know Miss Connolly very well. She begged me to undertake the complete management of Johnnywater ranch, and to that end she signed this Power of Attorney. You will see, Mr. Hawkins, that it has been duly certified and that the date is much earlier than your first knowledge of the place. Miss Connolly also gave me the deed and this certificate of the water rights. Everything is perfectly legal and straight, and I'm sorry to say—No, by heck, I'm not sorry! It's a relief to me to know that your contract isn't worth a lead nickel. In order to get this place on shares, you would need to make an agreement with me. And you would not get the terms Miss Connolly was so generous as to give you. One half the increase in stock, any loss in the old stock during the term of contract to be made good when you turned the place back to its owner, are the usual terms. Your expenses would not be paid for you.

"However, that is beside the point. I am not in favor of letting the place go on shares—not at present, anyway. So this is what you did not wait last night to hear."

"It's a frame-up!" snorted James Blaine Hawkins indignantly. "It's a rotten frame-up! I'll bet them papers is forged. There's a law made to handle just such cases as yours, young feller. And yuh needn't think I'm going to stand and be held up like that."

"Well, I've told you all you're entitled to know. I've no objection to your camping here for a while, so long as you behave yourself." Gary threw away his cigarette stub. His tone had been as casual as if he were gossiping with Monty, but was not so friendly. He really did not want to fight James Blaine Hawkins, in spite of the fact that he had discussed the possibility quite frankly with the cat.

But James Blaine Hawkins had spent an uncomfortable night and he wanted some one else to pay for it. He began to shake his fists and to call names, none of which were nice. Gary was up to something, and Hawkins was not going to stand for it, whatever it was. Gary was a faker, a thief—though what he had stolen James Blaine Hawkins failed to stipulate. Gary was a forger (Hawkins hinted darkly that he had, in some mysterious manner, evolved those papers during the night for the express purpose of using them as a bluff this morning) and he was also a liar.

Wherefore Gary reached out a long arm and slapped James Blaine Hawkins stingingly on the ear. When the head of James Blaine Hawkins snapped over to his right shoulder, Gary reached his other long arm and slapped the head upright. James Blaine Hawkins backed up and felt his ear; both ears, to be exact.

"I didn't come here to have no trouble," James Blaine Hawkins protested indignantly. "A man of brains can always settle things *with* his brains. I don't want to fight, and I ain't goin' to fight. I'm goin' to settle this thing——"

"With your brains. Well, go on and settle it then. Only be careful and don't sprain your head! Thinking's dangerous when you're not used to it. And if you do any more talking—which I certainly don't advise—be careful of the words you use, Mr. Hawkins. I'm not a liar or a thief. Don't call me either one."

James Blaine Hawkins spluttered and swore and argued one-sidedly. Gary leaned against the cabin with his arms folded negligently and listened with supreme indifference if one were to believe his manner.

"Rave on," he said indulgently. "Get it all out of your system—and then crank your little Ford and iris out of this scene, will you? I did say you could stay for a day or so if you behaved yourself. But you better beat it. The going may not be so good after awhile."

James Blaine Hawkins intimated that he would go when he got good and ready. So Gary went in and shut the door. He was sick of the fellow. The man was the weakest kind of a bully. He wouldn't fight. Heretofore Gary had believed that only a make-believe villain in a story would refuse to fight after he had been slapped twice.

When Gary came out of the cabin for a bucket of water, James Blaine Hawkins was fumbling in the car and talking to himself. He straightened up and renewed his aimless accusations when Gary passed him going to the creek.

The Voice suddenly shouted from the bluff, but Gary continued on his way, seemingly oblivious to the sound.

"Who's that hollerin' up there? Thought you said you was alone here. What does that feller want?" James Blaine Hawkins left the Ford and started after Gary.

"Beg pardon?" While the Voice continued to shout, Gary looked inquiringly at Hawkins.

"I asked yuh who was hollerin' up there! What does he want?"

Gary continued to look at James Blaine Hawkins. "Hollering?" His eyes narrowed a bit. "On the bluff, did you say?"

"Not over on *that* bluff," James Blaine Hawkins bellowed. "Up there, across the creek! Good Lord, are yuh deef? Can't yuh hear that hollering?"

Gary half turned his head and listened carefully. "Can you still hear it?" he asked in the midst of a loud halloo.

"You must be deef if *you* don't," James Blaine Hawkins spluttered.

Gary shook his head. "My hearing is splendid," he stated calmly. "I was a wireless operator on a sub-chaser during the war. Do you still hear it?"

James Blaine Hawkins testified profanely that he did. He was looking somewhat paler than was normal. He stared at Gary anxiously.

"What was that damfool yarn you was telling last night——"

"Oh, about the Indian that heard some one hollering on the bluff after Steve Carson disappeared? By Jove! I wonder if it can be the *Voice* you hear!" He looked at Hawkins blankly. "Say, I'm sorry I slapped you, Mr. Hawkins. I'd like to feel—afterwards—that you didn't hold any grudge against me for that." He held out his hand with the pitying smile of one who wishes to make amends before it is too late.

James Blaine Hawkins swallowed twice. Gary set down the bucket and laid a hand kindly on the man's shoulder.

"Aw, buck up, Mr. Hawkins. I—I guess they lied about that Injun dying right after—don't you believe it, anyway." And then, anxiously, "Do you still hear it, old fellow?"

Gary felt absolutely certain that James Blaine Hawkins did hear. Above the sound of the wind in the tree tops, the Voice was calling imperiously from the bluff.

"You can keep the damn place for all of me," James Blaine Hawkins exploded viciously. "I wouldn't have it as a gift. There's that damned cat I seen last night! A man's crazy that'd think of staying in a hole like this."

He was cranking furiously when Gary tapped him on the shoulder.

"Since you aren't going to stay and fulfill the contract," Gary said evenly, "you better hand over that two hundred dollars which Miss Connolly advanced you under the 'found' clause of your agreement. I'll give you a receipt for it, of course."

James Blaine Hawkins meant to refuse, but Gary's fingers slid up to his ear and pulled him upright.

"We'll just go in the cabin where I can write that receipt," he explained cheerfully, and led James Blaine Hawkins inside. "You're in a hurry to go, and I'm in a hurry to have you. So we'll make this snappy."

It must have been snappy indeed, for within five minutes James Blaine Hawkins was driving down the trail toward the mouth of the cañon, quite as fast as he had driven the night before. Only this time he went in broad daylight and he had no intention of ever coming back.

CHAPTER EIGHTEEN
GARY RIDES TO KAWICH

Gary saddled Jazz, filled the two canteens at the creek, tied some food for himself and rolled barley for Jazz in a flour sack—with a knot tied between to prevent mixing—and rode down the trail before the dust had fully settled after the passing of James Blaine Hawkins.

Primarily he wanted to make sure that Hawkins was actually leaving for town. After that he meant to ride over to Kawich, if he could find the place. In the mental slump that followed close on the heels of his altercation, Gary felt an overwhelming hunger for speech with a friend. Monty Girard was practical, wholesome and loyal as a man may be. Not for a long while had Gary known a man of Monty Girard's exact type. He confessed frankly to himself that certain phases of the James Blaine Hawkins incident had shaken his nerves. He was not at all sure that he meant to tell Monty about that side of the encounter, but he felt that he needed the mental tonic of Monty Girard's simple outlook on life. There was nothing subtle, no complexities in Monty's nature.

He dismounted and fastened the gate carefully behind him with a secret twist of the wire that would betray the fact if another opened the gate in his absence. As an added precaution he brushed out the trail of his own passing, as far as he could reach inside the gate with a pine branch. It was not likely that any one would visit Johnnywater Cañon; but Gary felt an unexplained desire to know it if they did. There was not one chance in a hundred that any one passing through the gate would observe the untracked space just within. An Indian might. But Gary had no fear that any Indian would invade Johnnywater Cañon. For that matter, it was not fear at all that impelled the caution. He simply wanted to know if any one visited the place.

Far down the mesa a cloud of gray dust rolled swiftly along a brown pencil-marking through the sage. That would be James Blaine Hawkins heading for Las Vegas as fast as gas and four cylinders would take him. Gary pulled up and watched the dust cloud, his eyes laughing.

"God bless that pinto cat!" he murmured, and leaned to smooth the sorrel's mane which the wind was tossing and tangling. "We won't see him again—for a while, anyway. But golly grandma, won't Pat be sore at the way I jimmed her revenge on Handsome Gary! But you know, Jazz, I expect to have to live with Pat, and I don't expect to do all my walking on my knees, either. A little demonstration of manly authority now and then does 'em good. They won't own it, Jazz, but they all like to feel they've tamed a cave man, and goodness knows when he may get rough. I worked in 'The Taming of the Shrew,' and I learned a lot about women from that."

The dust cloud rolled out of sight around a lonesome black butte, and Gary waved it a mocking farewell and got out the map which Monty had made of the trail to Kawich.

"Five miles down the trail toward town, and then turn short off to the left," he mumbled, studying the crude map. "That's simple enough—and no wonder I couldn't trail Monty afoot. I didn't walk to where he turned off. But hold on here! Dotted line shows faint stock trail straight across country to the Kawich road. Monty did say something about a cut-off, Jazz. All right, we'll hunt around here in the sage till we find that dotted line. This is great stuff. Feel so good now I don't have to go see Monty to get cheered up. But we'll go just the same—and see the country."

The trail, when he found it, was so faint that it was scarcely distinguishable in the gravelly soil. In places where they followed a rocky ridge Gary would have missed it altogether; but once on the trail Jazz followed it by instinct and his familiarity with the country. Probably he had traveled that way before, carrying Waddell, or perhaps Steve Carson, since Jazz was well past his youth.

Unconsciously Gary laid aside his movie habit of weaving in and out among the sage at a gallop, and dropped back into the old, shacking trail-trot he had learned from his father's riders. It was the gait to which Jazz was long accustomed, and it carried them steadily over the rough mesa to where the road angled off through the foothills.

The distant hills looked more unreal than ever. The clouds that grouped themselves around the violet-tinted peaks were like dabs of white paint upon a painted sky line. Again the sense of waiting in a tremendous calm impressed Gary with the immeasurable patience of the universe.

Insensibly the mental burden of loneliness, the nameless dread of things unseen and incomprehensible, lightened. The strained look left his eyes; the lines in his face relaxed as if he slept and, sleeping, forgot the worries of his waking hours. The world around him was so big, so quiet—the forces of nature were so invincible in their strength—that the cares of one small human being seemed as pettily unimportant as the scurrying of a lizard down the road. It occurred to Gary whimsically that the lizard's panicky retreat before the approaching cataclysm of the horse's shadow was very real and tremendously important—to the lizard. Quite as important, no doubt, as the complexity of emotions that filled the human soul of a certain Gary Marshall in Johnnywater Cañon. And the great butte that stood in its immutable strength under the buffetings of wind and sun and rain looked alike upon the troubles of the lizard and of Gary Marshall.

"After all, Jazz, we haven't got such a heck of a lot to worry about. If I was a jack rabbit I reckon I'd still have troubles of my own. Take your ears off your neck, Jazz, and shack along. Packing me over to Kawich isn't the worst thing could happen you, you lazy brute."

Gradually it dawned upon Gary that the road was creeping around the great butte that held Johnnywater Cañon gashed into the side turned toward the southeast. He wondered if the place called Kawich might not be just across the butte from Johnnywater. There was a certain comfort in the thought that Monty might not be so far from him, after all. Above him towered the bold outline of the butte, capped by the sheer wall of rock that rose like a cliff above its precipitous slopes. The trail itself followed the line of least resistance through the wrinkles formed in the foothills when this old world was cooling. But however deep the cañon, wherever the winding trail led, always the butte stood high-shouldered and grim just under the clouds. Gary could not wonder at the dilapidated condition of Monty's Ford, when he saw the trail it had been compelled to travel.

He ate his lunch beside a little spring that trickled out from beneath a rock just above the trail. Another hour's riding brought him into the very dooryard of a camp which he judged was Monty's, though no one appeared in answer to his call.

In point of picturesqueness and the natural beauty of its surroundings, Gary felt impelled to confide to Jazz that Johnnywater had Kawich beaten to a pulp. Kawich lacked the timber and the talkative little stream that distinguished Johnnywater Cañon. The camp itself was a rude shack built of boards and canvas, with a roof of corrugated iron and a sprinkle of tin cans and bits of broken implements surrounding it. The sun beat harshly down upon the barren knoll, and heat waves radiated from the iron roof. A cattle-trodden pathway led down to a zinc-lined trough in a hollow. The trough was full, with little lips of water pushing out over the edge here and there in a continuous drip-drip that muddied the ground immediately beneath the trough and made deep trampling tracks when the cattle crowded down to water. A crude corral was built above the trough, enclosing one end so that corralled stock could drink at will. The charred remains of the burnt Ford tilted crazily on the slope with its nose toward a brushy little gulch.

Gary took in all the bleak surroundings and the general air of discomfort that permeated the place. It struck him suddenly that Johnnywater Cañon was not so bad a place after all, with its whispery piñons, its picturesque log cabin set in the grove and the little gurgling stream just beyond. If it were not for the Voice and the eerie atmosphere of the place, he thought a person might rather enjoy a month or two there in the summer. Certainly it held more of the vacation elements than did this camp at Kawich.

He dismounted, led Jazz down into the corral, unsaddled him and left him to his own devices. There did not seem to be any feed about the place, and he was glad that he had brought plenty of grain for Jazz. He could do very well for twenty-four hours on rolled barley rations, Gary thought.

Monty could not be very far away, for he had eaten his breakfast there and had left cooked food covered under a cloth on the table for his next meal. As to the comforts of living, Monty seemed to be no better off than was Gary in Johnnywater Cañon. A camp bed in its canvas tarp was spread upon the board bunk in one corner of the shack. The cook stove was small and rusty from many rains that had beaten down through the haggled hole in the corrugated iron roof. The stovepipe was streaked with red lines of rust. There was the inevitable cupboard built of boxes nailed one above the other, bottoms against the wall. There was the regulation assortment of necessary supplies: coffee, salt, lard, a can of bacon grease, rice, sugar, beans and canned corn and tomatoes. Of reading matter, Monty seemed to have a little more than Waddell had left behind him. There was a small pile of *Stock Growers Journals*, some old Salt Lake papers and half a dozen old *Populars* with the backs torn off.

Gary chose a magazine that had a complete novel by an author whose work he liked. He stretched himself out on his back on the bunk, crossed his feet, wriggled his shoulders into a comfortable position just under Monty's only pillow, and in two sentences was away back in Texas after a mysterious gang of cattle rustlers.

CHAPTER NINETEEN
"HAVE YUH-ALL GOT A GUN?"

He was still hot on the trail and expecting every moment to have his horse shot from under him, when Monty pulled open the door and walked in upon him, swearing affectionately. Gary sat up, turned down a corner of the page to mark his place, and reached for his smoking material.

"Golly grandma, I meant to have supper ready!" he exclaimed. "But I got to reading and forgot all about eating."

"How yuh-all been making out?" Monty wanted to know. "Going to catch a ride back to town?"

Gary licked the cigarette paper and shook his head while he pressed it into place. "No, the action is just beginning to get snappy now," he said.

"Meanin' what?" Monty paused in the act of lifting a stove lid.

"Meaning that I just put on a fight scene, and ran the heavy clean out of the cañon as per usual."

"Yeah?" Monty's tone betrayed a complete lack of understanding.

"You bet. Never saw a leading man get licked, did you? I'm starring in this piece—so naturally I just *had* to put the heavy on the run."

"What's a heavy?"

"The villain. Pat Connolly went and had another impulse. She let the place on shares to a gink that I'll bet has done time. He had every mark of a crook, and he had the darndest holdup game you ever saw. Pat Connolly doesn't know anything at all about ranches. She went and——"

"Pat Connolly—*she?*" Monty was dipping cold water into the coffeepot, and he spilled a cupful.

"Er—yes." Gary reddened a bit. "She's a girl all right. Finest in the world. Patricia Connolly's her name, and if I can pull her clear on this damned Johnnywater investment and remain on speaking terms with Pat, I expect she'll become Mrs. Marshall. She's not at all like other girls, Monty. Pat's got brains. A crackerjack stenographer and bookkeeper. Got a man-sized job with the Consolidated Grain and Milling Company in the city. You may have heard of them."

"Sure," said Monty. "Sent there once for some oil cakes to winter my she stock on. Costs too much, though. A cow ain't worth what it costs to feed one through the winter. What about this feller yuh run off?"

Gary got up and began helping with the supper while he told all about James Blaine Hawkins and his AGREEMENT OF CONTRACT.

Monty was in the position of a man who dips into the middle of a story and finds it something of a jumble because he does not know what went before. He asked a good many questions, so that the telling lasted through supper and the dishwashing afterwards. By the time they were ready to sit down and smoke with the comfortable assurance that further exertion would not be necessary that night, Monty was pretty well up-to-date on the affairs of Gary Marshall and Patricia Connolly, up to and including the arrival of James Blaine Hawkins at Johnnywater and his hurried departure that morning.

"And yuh-all say the feller seen something," Monty drawled meditatively after a minute or two of silence. "Did he tell yuh what it was he saw?"

"No, except that he thought it was a man who had slipped into the cabin when he wasn't looking. But it was the cat that really put him on the run. Seems he hated to see a cat unless I saw it too."

Monty looked up quickly. In Gary's tone he had caught a certain reluctance to speak of the man which James Blaine Hawkins declared he saw. He was willing enough to explain all about James Blaine Hawkins and the cat, and he had laughed when he told how he had pretended not to hear the Voice. But of the possible apparition of a man Gary did not like to talk.

"Tell the truth, now—ain't yuh scared to stay there alone?" Monty's question was anxious.

Gary shrugged his shoulders and blew a smoke ring, watching it drift up toward the ceiling. "Being scared or not being scared makes no difference whatever. I'm going to stay. For a while, anyway."

"I wisht you'd tell me what for," Monty urged uneasily. "A man that can hold down the position and earn the money yuh did in pictures kain't afford to set around in Johnnywater Cañon lookin' after two shoats and a dozen or fifteen hens. I don't agree with Miss Connolly at all. I'd be mighty proud if I could do what I've seen yuh-all do in pictures. Your actin' was real—and I reckon that's what puts a man at the top. I know the top-notchers all act so good you kain't ketch 'em at it. Yuh just seem to be lookin' in on 'em whilst they're livin'."

"The best acting I've done," chuckled Gary, "was last night and this morning. I was scared to death that the pinto cat would come and hop up on my lap like she usually does. I'd have had a merry heck of a time acting like she wasn't there. But I put it over—enough to send him breezing down the cañon, anyway."

"You're liable to have trouble with that feller yet," warned Monty. "If he got an agreement out of Miss Connolly, he ain't liable to give up the idea of holding her to it. Have yuh-all got a gun?"

"An automatic, yes." Gary pulled the gun from his hip pocket. "I carry this just in case. I was born and raised where men pack guns—but they didn't ride with 'em cocked and in their hands ready to shoot, like we do in the movies. There's a lot of hokum I do before the camera that gives me a pain. So if I should happen to need a gun, I've got one. But don't you worry about James Blaine Hawkins. *He* won't show up again."

"I wouldn't be none too sure of that," Monty reiterated admonishingly. "He's liable to get to thinkin' it over in town and git his courage back. Things like Johnnywater has got don't look so important when you're away off somewhere just thinkin' about it."

"I guess you're right, at that," Gary admitted. "He'll probably get over the cat and the Voice, all right, and—that other spell of imagination. But without meaning to brag on myself, I think he'll study it over a while before he comes around trying to bully me again. You see, Monty, the man's an awful coward. I slapped him twice and even then he wouldn't fight. He just backed up away from me and cooled right down."

"Them's the kind uh skunks yuh want to look out for," Monty declared sententiously.

But Gary only laughed at him and called him the original gloom, and insisted upon talking of something altogether different.

Monty, it transpired, had promised to help a man through haying over in Pahranagat Valley and meant to start the next day. He was frankly relieved to know that Gary was still all right. He had wanted to ride over to Johnnywater again before going to Pahranagat, but had had too much riding of his own to do.

"But if you're bent on hangin' out there," he said, after some futile argument, "I'll ride on over when I get through with this job. What yuh-all trying to do over there, anyway? Hate yourself to death?"

"Well, I hope I'm pleasing Pat," Gary laughed evasively.

"Well, I hate to be butting in," Monty said diffidently, "but if she wanted yuh to stay over here and run Johnnywater, it don't seem to me like she'd 'a' sent this Hawkins feller over with a five years' contract to run the place on shares. Didn't she send yuh no word about why she done it?"

"She did not! I have a hunch Pat's pretty sore at me. You see, she sprung this deal on me kinda sudden, right on top of a strawberry shortcake when I didn't want to think. I told her what I thought about it—and I told it straight. So we had a little—er—argument. She up and threw my profile in my face, and called me flabby souled. So I up and left. And I didn't go back to tell her good-by when I started over here, so I wouldn't be surprised if little Pat Connolly is pretty well peeved."

Monty smoked and studied the matter. "Does she know you're over here?" he asked abruptly. "Seems kinda funny to me, that she'd go and send Hawkins over here without sayin' a word to yuh about it. She could 'a' wrote, couldn't she? If yuh-all didn't tell her yuh was coming, how would she know yuh was here?"

"Why, she could call up the studio and get the dope from Mills, my director," Gary explained uncomfortably.

"But would she? Seems like as if *I* was a girl and had any spunk, I wouldn't want to let on that the feller I was engaged to had gone off somewheres without letting me know about it."

"That's one way to look at it," Gary admitted. "But Pat's nobody's fool. She could find out all right, without letting on."

"Well, it's none of my put-in—but I don't reckon yuh-all are pleasing Pat Connolly much by sticking over here."

Gary got up and stretched his arms above his head. "She wanted me to sit in my cabin and listen to a saddle horse champing hay," he contended lightly. "I think I'll go down and give Jazz a feed of barley to champ."

Monty understood quite well that Gary meant to end the discussion right there. He said no more about it, therefore. But he promised himself—and mentally he promised Patricia as well—that he would manage somehow to bring about a complete understanding between these two obstinate young people.

They slept shoulder to shoulder that night in Monty's bunk, and the next morning they saddled early and each rode his way, feeling the better for the meeting.

CHAPTER TWENTY
"THAT CAT AIN'T HUMAN!"

Monty rode rather anxiously into Johnnywater Cañon, determined to take whatever means he found necessary to persuade Gary to return to Los Angeles and "make it up with his girl." With three weeks' wages in his pocket Monty felt sufficiently affluent to buy the pigs and chickens if Gary used them for a point in his argument against going.

Monty had spent a lot of time during those three weeks in mulling over in his mind the peculiar chain of circumstances that had dragged Gary to Johnnywater. What bond it was that held him there, Monty would have given much to know. He was sure that Gary disliked the place, and that he hated to stay there alone. It seemed unreasonable that any normal young man would punish himself like that from sheer stubbornness; yet Gary would have had Monty believe that he was staying to spite Patricia.

Monty did not believe it. Gary had shown himself to be too intelligent, too level-headed and safely humorous in his viewpoints to harbor that peculiar form of egotism. Monty was shrewd enough to recognize the fact that "cutting off the nose to spite the face" is a sport indulged in only by weak natures who own an exaggerated ego. Wherefore, Gary failed to convince him that he was of that type of individual.

At the same time, he could think of no other reason that could possibly hold a man like Gary Marshall at Johnnywater. Monty had a good memory for details. Certain trivial incidents he remembered vividly: Gary's stealthy approach around the corner of the cabin with the upraised pitchfork in his hands; Gary's forced gayety afterwards, and the strained look in his eyes—the lines beside the mouth; Gary's reluctance to speak of the uncanny, nameless *something* that clung to Johnnywater Cañon; the incomprehensible behavior of the spotted cat. And always Monty brought up short with a question which he asked himself but could not answer.

Why had Gary Marshall described Steven Carson—who had dropped from sight of mortal eyes five years and more ago?—why had Gary described Steve Carson and asked if that description fitted Waddell?

"Gary never saw Steve Carson—not when he was alive, anyway. He says the Indians never told him how Steve looked. I reckon he really thought Waddell was that kind uh lookin' man. But how in thunder did he *get the idea?*" Monty frequently found himself mentally asking that question, but he never attempted to put an answer into words. He couldn't. He didn't know the answer.

So here he was, peering anxiously at the cabin squatted between the two great piñon trees in the grove and hoping that Gary was still all right. He had consciously put aside an incipient dread of James Blaine Hawkins and his possible vengefulness toward Gary. Monty told himself that there was no use in crossing that bridge until he came to it. He had come over for the express purpose of offering to take the Walking X cattle on shares and look after them with his own. He would manage somehow to take charge of the pigs and chickens as well. He decided that he could kill the pigs and pack the meat over on his horse. And he could carry the chickens on a pack horse in a couple of crates. There would be nothing then to give Gary any excuse for staying.

Remembering how he had startled Gary before with calling, Monty did not dismount at the cabin. Instead, he rode close to the front window, leaned and peered in like an Indian; and finding the cabin empty, he went on through the grove to the corral. Jazz was there, standing hip-shot in a shady corner next the creek, his head nodding jerkily while he dozed. Monty's horse whinnied a greeting and Jazz awoke with a start and came trotting across the corral to slide his nose over the top rail nearest them.

Monty rode on past the potato patch and the alfalfa meadow where a second crop was already growing apace. There was no sign of Gary, and Monty rode on to the very head of the cañon and back to the cabin.

A vague uneasiness seized Monty in spite of his efforts to throw it off. Gary should be somewhere in the cañon, since he would not leave it afoot, not while he had a horse doing nothing in the corral. Of course, if anything were wrong with Jazz——Monty turned and rode back to the corral, where he dismounted by the gate. He went in and walked up to Jazz, and examined him with the practiced palms of the expert horseman. He slapped Jazz on the rump and shooed him around the corral at a lope.

"There ain't a thing in the world the matter with *you*," he told the horse, after a watchful minute or two. Then he rolled a cigarette, lighted and smoked it while he waited and meditated upon the probable whereabouts of Gary.

He went out into the open and studied the steep bluff sides, foot by foot. The entire width of the cañon was no more than a long rifle-shot. If Gary were climbing anywhere along its sides, Monty would be able to see him. But there was no sign of movement anywhere, though he took half an hour for the examination.

He returned to the cabin, leaving his horse in the corral with saddle and bridle off and a forkful of hay under his eager nose. He shouted Gary's name.

"Hey, *Gary! Oh-h-h*, Gary!" he called, over and over, careful to enunciate the words.

From high up on the bluff somewhere the Voice answered him mockingly, shouting again and again a monotonous, eerie call. There was no other sound for a time, and Monty went into the cabin to see if he could find there some clue to Gary's absence.

Little things bear a message plain as print to those dwellers of the wilderness who depend much upon their eyes and their ears. The cabin told Monty with absolute certainty that Gary had not planned an absence of more than a few hours at most. Nor had he left in any great haste. He had been gone, Monty judged, since breakfast. Of the cooked food set away in the cupboard, two pancakes lay on top of a plate containing three slices of fried bacon. To Monty that meant breakfast cleared away and no later meal prepared. He looked at his watch. He had taken an early start from Kawich, and it was now two o'clock.

He lifted the lid of the stove and reached in, feeling the ashes. There had been no fire since morning; he was sure of that. He stood in the middle of the room and studied the whole interior questioningly. Gary's good clothes—which were not nearly so good as they had been when Monty first saw him—hung against the wall farthest from the stove, the coat neatly spread over a makeshift hanger. Gary's good hat was in the cupboard nailed to the wall. A corner of his suit case protruded from under the bunk. Gary was in the rough clothes he had gleaned from Waddell's leavings.

Monty could not find any canteen, but that told him nothing at all. He could not remember whether Waddell had canteens or not. The vague uneasiness which he had at first smothered under his natural optimism grew to a definite anxiety. He knew the ways of the desert. And he could think of no plausible reason why Gary should have left the cañon afoot.

He went out and began looking for tracks. The dry soil still held the imprint of automobile tires, but it was impossible to tell just how long ago they had been made. Several days, at least, he judged after a careful inspection. He heard a noise in the bushes across the little creek and turned that way expectantly.

The spotted cat came out of the brush, jumped the tiny stream and approached him, meowing dolefully. Monty stood stock still, watching her advance. She came directly toward him, her tail drooping and waving nervously from side to side. She looked straight up into his face and yowled four or five times without stopping.

"Get out, damn yuh!" cried Monty and motioned threateningly with his foot. "Yuh can't stand there and yowl at *me*—I got enough on my mind right now."

The mottled cat ducked and started back to the creek, stopping now and then to look over her shoulder and yowl at Monty. Monty picked up a pebble and shied it after her. The cat gave a final squall and ran into a clump of bushes a few yards up-stream from where Monty had first seen her.

"That damned cat ain't human!" Monty ejaculated uncomfortably. "That's the way she yowled around when Steve Carson———" He lifted his shoulders impatiently at the thought.

After a minute or two spent in resisting the impulse, Monty yielded and started out to see where the cat had gone. Beyond the clump of bushes lay an open space along the bank of the creek. On the farther side he saw the mottled cat picking her way through weeds and small bushes, still going up the creek and yowling mournfully as she went. Monty walked slowly after her. He noticed, while he was crossing the open space, a man's footprints going that way and another set coming back. The soil was too loose to hold a clear imprint, so that Monty could not tell whose tracks they were; though he believed them to have been made by Gary.

The cat looked back and yowled at Monty, then went on. At a point nearly opposite the potato patch the cat stopped near a bushy little juniper tree that stood by itself where the creek bank rounded up to a tiny knoll. As Monty neared the spot the cat leaped behind the juniper and disappeared.

Monty went closer, stopped with a jerk and stood staring. He felt his knees quiver with a distinct tendency to buckle under him. The blood seeped slowly away from his face, leaving it sallow under the tan.

Monty was standing at the very edge of a narrow mound of earth that still bore the marks of a shovel where the mound had been smoothed and patted into symmetrical form. A grave, the length of a man.

Here again were the blurred footprints in the loose soil. Who had made them, what lay buried beneath that narrow ridge of heaped sand, Monty shrank from conjecturing.

With an involuntary movement, of which Monty was wholly unconscious, his right hand went up to his hat brim. He stood there for a space without moving. Then he turned and almost ran to the corral. It was not until he reached to open the gate that Monty discovered his hat in his hand.

He was thinking swiftly now, holding his thoughts rigidly to the details of what he must do. The name Hawkins obtruded itself frequently upon his mind, but he pushed the thought of Hawkins from him. Beyond the details of his own part, which he knew he must play unfalteringly from now on, he would not think—he could not bear to think. He saddled Jazz, mounted and led his own horse down to the cabin. Working swiftly, he packed a few blankets, food for three days and his own refilled canteens upon the led horse.

Then with a last shrinking glance around the cañon walls, he mounted Jazz. He remembered then something that he must do, something that Gary would wish to have him do. He rode back to the stone pen and opened the gate so that the pigs could run free and look after themselves.

He remounted, then half-turned in the saddle and took up the slack in the lead rope, got the led horse straightened out behind him and kicked Jazz into a trot. In his mental stress he loped the horses all the way down to the cañon's mouth. And then, striking into the dim trail, he went racking away over the small ridges and into the hollows, heading straight for the road most likely to be traveled in this big, empty land; the road that stretched its long, long miles between Goldfield and Las Vegas.

CHAPTER TWENTY-ONE
GARY FOLLOWS THE PINTO CAT

Gary had prospected pretty thoroughly the whole cañon, following the theory that some one—he felt that it was probably Steve Carson—had carried that rich, gold-bearing rock down to the cabin. Waddell had left neither chemicals nor appliances by which he could test any of the mineralized rock he found; but Gary was looking for one particular kind, the porphyry that carried free gold.

Greater than the loneliness, stronger than his dread of the cañon and the cabin, was his desire to find more of that gold-bearing rock. It would not take much of it to make Pat's investment in Johnnywater more than profitable. He even climbed to the top of the butte—a heart-breaking effort accomplished at the risk of his neck on the sheer wall of the rim rock. There was no means of knowing just where that porphyry had come from. In some prehistoric eruption it might have been thrown for miles, though Gary did not believe that it had been. The top of the bluff gave no clue whatever. Malapi bowlders strewed much of the surface with outcroppings of country rock. Certainly there was no sign of mineral up there. He tramped the butte for miles, however, and spent two days in doing it. Then, satisfied that the porphyry must be somewhere in the cañon, he renewed his search on the slope.

Prospecting here was quite as difficult, because so much of the upper slopes was covered with an overburden of the malapi that formed the rim rock. Portions of the rim would break and slide when the storms beat upon it. Considerable areas of loose rock had formed during the centuries of wear and tear, and if there had been mineral outcroppings they were as effectually hidden as if they had never come to the surface at all. But a strain of persistence which Gary had inherited from pioneering forebears held him somewhat doggedly to the search.

He reasoned that he had more time than he knew what to do with, and if a fortune were hidden away in this cañon, it would be inexcusable for him to mope through the days without making any systematic effort to find it. Patricia deserved the best fortune the world had to bestow. To find one for her would, he told himself whimsically, wipe out the stain of owning a profile and a natural marcel wave over his temples. Pat might possibly forgive even his painted eyebrows and painted lashes and painted lips, if he found her a gold mine.

So he tramped and scrambled and climbed from one end of the cañon walls to the other, and would not hint to Monty Girard what it was that held him in Johnnywater Cañon. He would not even put his hopes on paper in the long, lonely evenings when he wrote to Patricia. After the jibing letter concerning the millions she might have if she owned a mine as rich as the rock he had found behind the cabin, Gary had not put his search into words even when he talked to Faith.

He found himself thinking more and more about Steve Carson. The weak-souled Waddell he had come practically to ignore. Waddell had left no impress upon the cañon, at least, so far as Gary was concerned. And that in spite of the fact that he was walking about in Waddell's boots and trousers, wearing Waddell's hat, tending Waddell's pigs. Walking in Waddell's boots, Gary wondered about Steve Carson, speculated upon his life and his hopes and the things he had put away in his past when he came to Johnnywater to live alone, wholly apart from his fellows. Steve Carson's hands had built the cabin between the two piñons. Steve Carson—Gary did not attempt any explanation of why he knew it was so—had brought the gold-bearing rock to the cabin. A prospector of sorts, he must have been, to have found gold-bearing rock in that cañon.

It was during the forenoon after Gary had returned from Kawich that he obeyed a sudden, inexplicable impulse to follow Faith, the mottled cat.

Ever since Gary had come to Johnnywater he had seen Faith go off across the creek after breakfast. Usually she returned in the course of three or four hours, and frequently she brought some small rodent or a bird home with her. Gary had been faintly amused by the pinto cat's regular hours and settled habits of living. He used to compliment her upon her decorous behavior, stroking her back while she purred on his knee, her paws tucked snugly close to her body.

On this morning Gary rose abruptly from the doorstep, and, bareheaded, he followed Faith across the creek and up the bluff. It was hot climbing, but Gary did not think about the heat. Indeed, he was not consciously thinking of anything much. He was simply following Faith up the bluff, because he had got up from the doorstep to follow Faith.

Faith climbed up and up quite as if she knew exactly where she was going. Gary, stopping once on a bowlder to breathe for a minute after an unusually stiff bit of climbing, saw the cat look up in the queer way she had of doing. In a minute she went on and Gary followed.

It began to look as if Faith meant to climb to the top of the butte. She made her way around the lower edge of a slide, went out of sight into a narrow gulch which Gary, with all his prospecting had never noticed before—or at least had never entered—and reappeared farther up, just under the rim rock where many slides had evidently had their birth. For the first time since he had left the cabin, the cat looked back at Gary, gave an amiable mew and waited a minute before she started on.

Gary hesitated. He was thirsty, and the rapid climb was beginning to tell on him. He looked back down the bluff to the cool green of the grove, and for the first time wondered why he had been such a fool as to follow a cat away up here on a hunting trip in which he could not possibly take any active interest or part. He told himself what a fool he was and said he must be getting goofy himself. But when he moved it was upward, after the cat.

He brought up at the foot of a high ledge seamed and cracked as one would never suspect, looking up from below. It was up here somewhere that the Voice always seemed to be located. He stopped and listened, but the whole cañon lay in a somnolent calm under the mounting sun. It looked as if nothing could disturb it; as if there never could be a Voice other than the everyday voices of men. While he stood there wiping his forehead and panting with the heat and the labor of climbing, the red rooster down in the grove began to crow lustily. The sound came faintly up to Gary, linking him lightly to commonplace affairs.

A little distance away the cat had curled herself down in a tiny hollow at the edge of the slide. Gary made his way over to her. She opened one eye and regarded him sleepily, gave a lazy purr or two and settled herself again more comfortably. Gary saw, from certain small scratchings in the gravel, that the pinto cat had made this little nest for herself. She had not been hunting at all. She had come to a spot with which she was very familiar.

CHAPTER TWENTY-TWO
THE PAT CONNOLLY MINE

Gary decided offhand that he had been neatly sold. He sat down on the loose rubble near Faith and made himself a smoke. The grove and the cabin were hidden from him by the narrow little ridge that looked perfectly smooth from the cañon bottom. But the rest of the cañon—the corral, the potato patch, the alfalfa—lay blocked out in miniature far below him. He stared down upon the peaceful picture it made and wondered why he had climbed all the way up here just following the pinto cat. For the matter of that, his following the cat was not half so purposeless as the cat's coming had been.

He looked down at her curled asleep in her little hollow. It struck him that this must have been her destination each time she crossed the creek and started up the bluff. But why should the cat come away up here every day? Gary did not attempt to explain the vagaries of a cat so eccentric as Faith had proved herself to be. He wondered idly if he were becoming eccentric also, just from constant association with Faith.

He laughed a little to himself and picked up a piece of malapi rock; balanced it in his hand while he thought of other things, and tossed it down the slide. It landed ten feet below him and began rolling farther, carrying with it a small avalanche of loose rocks. Gary watched the slide with languid interest. Even so small a thing could make a tiny ripple in the dead calm of the cañon that day.

The slide started by that one rock spread farther. Other rocks loosened and went rolling down the bluff, and Gary's eyes followed them and went higher, watching to see where next a rock would slip away from the mass and go rolling down. It seemed to him that the whole slide might be easily set in motion with no more than a kick or two at the top. He got up and began to experiment, kicking a rock loose here and there. There was no danger to himself, since he stood at the top of the slide. As for Faith, she had sprung up in a furry arch at the first slithering clatter and was now viewing the scene with extreme disfavor from the secure vantage point of a shelf on the ledge above Gary.

In a very few minutes Gary had set the whole surface of the slide in motion. The noise it made pleased him immensely. It served to break that waiting silence in the cañon. When the rocks ceased rolling, he started others. Finally he found himself standing upon firm ground again, with an outcropping of gray quartz just below him. His eyes fixed themselves upon the quartz in a steady stare before he dug heels into the slope and edged down to it.

With a malapi rock bigger than his two fists he hammered off a piece of quartz and held it in the shade of his body while he examined it closely. He turned it this way and that, fearful of deceiving himself by the very strength of his desire. But all the while he knew what were those little yellow specks that gleamed in the shade.

He knelt and pounded off other pieces of the quartz and compared them anxiously with the first. They were all identical in character: steel gray, with here and there the specks of gold in the gray, and the chocolate brown streaks and splotches of hematite—the "red oxide" iron which runs as high as seventy per cent. iron. Hematite and free gold in gray quartz——

"A prettier combination for free gold I couldn't have made to order!" he whispered, almost as if he were praying. "It's good enough for my girl's 'million-dollar mine'—though they *do* get rich off a piece of gold float in the movies!" He began to laugh nervously. A weaker-souled man would probably have wept instead.

With the side of his foot he tore away the rubble from the quartz outcropping. There, just where he had been kneeling, he discovered a narrow vein of the bird's-eye porphyry such as he had found at the cabin. Here, then, lay the object of all his tiresome prospecting. So far as he could judge, with only his hands and feet for digging, the vein averaged about eight inches in width. Whether the porphyry formed a wall for the quartz he could not tell at the surface; but he hoped fervently that it did. With hematite, gray quartz and bird's-eye porphyry he would have the ideal combination for a rich, permanent gold mine. And Pat, he reflected breathlessly, might really have her millions after all.

He picked up what he believed to be average samples of the vein and started back down the bluff, his imagination building air castles, mostly for Patricia. If he dramatized the event and cast himself for the leading man playing opposite Patricia, who was the star, surely he had earned the right to paint rose tints across the veil that hid his future and hers.

He had forgotten all about the cat; but when he reached the cabin, there she was at his heels looking extremely self-satisfied and waving her tail with a gentle air of importance. Gary laid his ore samples on the table and stood with his hands on his hips, looking down at Faith with a peculiar expression in his eyes. Suddenly he smiled endearingly at the cat, stooped and picked her up, holding her by his two hands so that he could look into her eyes.

"Doggone you, Faith, I wish to heck you could talk! I wouldn't put it past you to think like humans. I'll bet you've been trying all along to show me that outcropping. And I thought you were hunting mice and birds and gophers just like a plain, ordinary cat! You can't tell *me*—you knew all about that gold!

I'll bet you've got a name all picked out for the mine, too. But it won't go, I'll tell a meddlesome world. That is, unless you've decided it ought to be called 'The Pat Connolly.' Because that's the way it's going on record, if Handsome Gary has anything to say about it—and I rather think he has!"

Faith blinked at him and mewed understandingly. Gary wooled her a bit and put her down, considerately smoothing down the fur he had roughed. Faith was a forgiving cat, and she immediately began purring under his fingers. After that she tagged him indefatigably while he got mortar, pestle and pan, and carried them down to a shady spot beside the creek.

Gary's glance strayed often to the bluff while he broke bits off each sample of quartz and dropped them into the iron mortar. Then, with the mortar held firmly between his knees, Gary picked up the eight-inch length of iron with the round knob on the end and began to pulverize the ore. For a full quarter of an hour the quiet air of the grove throbbed to the steady *pung, pung, pung,* of the iron pestle striking upon rock particles in the deep iron bowl.

About twice in every minute, Gary would stop, dip thumb and finger into the mortar, and bring up a pinch of pulverized rock at which he would squint with the wholly unconscious eagerness of a small boy. Naturally, since he was not flattening a nugget of solid gold in the mortar, he failed to see anything except once when he caught an unmistakable yellow gleam from a speck of gold almost half the size of a small pinhead.

He gloated over that speck for a full minute before he shook it carefully back into the mortar. And then you should have heard him pound!

He was all aquiver with hope and eager expectancy when at last he poured the pulverized quartz into the gold pan and went digging his heels down the bank to the water. Faith came forward and stood upon a dry rock, mewing and purring by turns, and waving her tail encouragingly while she watched him.

Those who plod along the beaten trail toward commercial success can scarcely apprehend the thrill of winning from nature herself the symbol that promises fulfillment of hope and dreams coming true. The ardency of Gary's desire was measurable only by the depth of his love for Patricia. For himself he had a man's normal hunger for achievement. To discover a gold mine here in Johnnywater Cañon, to develop it in secret to the point where he could command what capital he needed for the making of a real mine, that in itself seemed to Gary a goal worth striving for. To fill Patricia's hands with virgin gold which he had found for her, there spoke the primitive desire of man since the world was young; to bring the spoils of war or the chase and lay them, proud offering of love, at the feet of his Woman.

Gary turned and tilted the pan, tenderly as a young mother cradles her first-born. He dipped and rocked and spilled the water carefully over the rim; dipped and rocked and tilted again. The three deep creases stood between his straight, dark eyebrows, but now they betokened eager concentration upon his work. At last, he poured clear water from the pan carefully, almost drop by drop. He tilted the pan slowly in the sunlight and bent his head, peering sharply into the pan. His heart seemed to be beating in his throat when he saw the trail of tiny yellow particles following sluggishly the spoonful of black sand when he tilted the pan.

"I've got it, Steve," he exclaimed, looking up over his shoulder. He caught his breath in the sudden realization that he was looking into the empty sunlight. Absorbed as he had been in the gold, the felt presence of Steve Carson looking over his shoulder had seemed perfectly natural and altogether real.

The momentary shock sobered him. But the old dread of that felt presence no longer assailed him as something he must combat by feigning unconsciousness. The unreasoning impression that Steve Carson—the mind of him—was there just behind his shoulder, watching and sharing in his delight, persisted nevertheless. Gary caught himself wondering if the thing was really only a prank of his imagination. Feeling a bit foolish, but choosing to indulge the whimsy, he stood up and turned deliberately, the pan held out before him.

"Steve Carson, if dead people go on living and thinking, and if you really are hanging around just out of sight but watching the game, I'm here to say that I hope you're glad I found this vein. And I want to tell you right now that if there's any money to be made out of it, it's going to the finest, squarest little girl in the world. So if there is such a thing as a spirit, just take it from me everything's going to be on the square."

He carried the pan up to the cabin and carefully rinsed the gold down into a jelly glass. He made no apology to himself for the little speech to a man dead and gone these five years. Having made himself as clear on the subject as was diplomatic—supposing Steve Carson's spirit had been present and could hear—he felt a certain relief and could lay the subject aside and devote himself to the fascination of hunting the gold out of the hills where it had lain buried for ages.

It occurred to him that he might find some particularly rich specimens, mortar them by hand and pan them for Patricia. A wedding ring made from the first gold taken and panned by hand—the hand of Gary Marshall—from "The Pat Connolly" mine, appealed to him irresistibly. Before he had mortared a lump of porphyry the size of a pigeon's egg, Gary had resolved to pan enough gold for that very purpose. He pictured himself pulling the ring from his vest pocket while the minister waited. He experienced a prophetic thrill of ecstasy when he slipped the ring upon Patricia's finger. The dreamed sentence, "I now pronounce you man and wife," intoned by an imaginary minister, thrilled him to the soul.

Pung, pung, pung! It wouldn't take so very long, if he mortared rock evenings, say, instead of killing time minute by minute playing solitaire with the deck of cards Waddell had thumbed before him. *Pung, pung, pung!* He could mortar the quartz in the evenings and pan it in the morning before he went to work. *Pung, pung, pung, pung!* He would hunt up a cow's horn and fix it as he had seen old prospectors do, so that he could blow the sand from the panned gold and carry it unmixed to the jeweler. *Pung, pung!* The porphyry sample was fine as corn meal under the miniature stamp-mill of Gary's pounding.

He was mighty careful of that handful of pulp. He even dipped the mortar half full of water and sloshed it round and round, pouring it afterward into the pan to rinse out what gold may have stuck to the iron. His finger tips stirred the wet mass caressingly in the pan, muddying the water with the waste matter and pouring that out before he squatted on his heels at the edge of the stream.

The result was gratifying in the extreme. Granting that the values were inclined to "jump" from quartz to porphyry and back again to the quartz, he would still lose none of the gold. He tried to be very conservative in estimating the probable value of the vein. He knew that, granting quartz and porphyry were in place from the surface downward, the values should increase with depth. It would take some digging, however, to determine that point. He was glad that Patricia knew nothing at all about it. If there were to be disappointment later on, he wanted to bear it alone. The joys of success he was perfectly willing to share; but not the sickening certitude of failure. He judged that the outcropping would run several hundred dollars to the ton, provided his panned samples had run a fair average of the vein.

Material for air castles aplenty, that! Gary was afraid to believe it. He kept warning himself headily that the world would be peopled entirely with multimillionaires if every man's dream of wealth came true and every man's hopes were realized.

"Ninety-nine per cent. of all mineral prospects are failures, Faith," he told the spotted cat admonishingly. "We may get the raspberry yet on this proposition. I'm just waiting to see whether you're a mascot or a jinx. I wish to heck you were a dog—I'd make you get busy and help dig!"

CHAPTER TWENTY-THREE
GARY FINDS THE VOICE—AND SOMETHING ELSE

"Here's where Handsome Gary raises a crop of callouses big as birds' eggs in his mad pursuit of the fickle jade, Fortune. Come on, Faith, doggone you; I want you handy in case this gold thing is a fluke."

Gary had remembered that eating is considered necessary to the preservation of life and had delayed his further investigation of the outcropping until he had scrambled together some sort of a meal. He had bolted food as if he must hurry to catch a train that was already whistling a warning. Now he took down a canteen from behind the door, shouldered an old pick and shovel he had found in the shed, and started back up the bluff, stopping just long enough to fill the canteen at the creek as he passed.

Loaded with canteen and tools, the climb was a heart-breaking one. The spotted cat led the way, going as straight as possible toward the tiny ridge behind which lay the outcropping. At the top, Gary decided that hereafter he would bring a lunch and spend the day up there, thus saving a valuable hour or two and a good deal of energy. Energy, he realized, would be needed in unlimited quantities if he did much development work alone.

By hard labor he managed to clear away the rubble of the slide and uncover the vein for a distance of several feet before dusk began to fill the cañon. He carried down with him the richest pieces of rock that he could find, and that night he worked with mortar and pestle until his arms ached with the unaccustomed exercise.

Several times that evening he was pulled away from his air castles by the peculiar sensation of some one standing very close to him. It was not the first time he had experienced the sensation, but never before had the impression brought him a comforting sense of friendly companionship. It struck him suddenly that he must be growing used to the idea, and that Johnnywater Cañon was not at all likely to "get" him as it had got Waddell. He had not heard the Voice all day, but he believed that he could now listen to it with perfect equanimity.

He had just one worry that evening; rather, he had one difficult problem to solve. In order to work in that quartz, dynamite was absolutely necessary. Unless he could find some on the place, it began to look very much as if he would not be able to do much unless he could get some brought out to him from town.

The result of his cogitations that evening was a belief that Steve Carson must have had dynamite, caps and fuse on hand. Men living out in a country known to produce minerals of one sort and another usually were supplied with explosives. Even if they never did any mining, they might want to blow a bowlder out of the way now and then. He had never seen any powder about the place; but on the other hand, he had not looked for any.

The next morning he panned the pulped rock immediately after breakfast and was overjoyed at the amount of gold he gleaned from the pint or so of pulp. At that rate, he told himself gleefully, the wedding ring would not need to wait very long. After that he went hunting dynamite in the storehouse and shed. He was lucky enough to find a couple of dozen sticks of powder and some caps and fuse wrapped in a gunny sack and hung from the ridgepole of the shed. The dynamite did not look so very old, and he guessed that it had been brought there by Waddell. This seemed to him an amazing bit of good luck, and he shouldered the stuff and went off up the bluff with an extra canteen and his lunch, whistling in an exuberance of good humor with the world. Faith, of course, went with him and curled herself in her little hollow just under the frowning malapi ledge.

Gary worked for three days, following the quartz and porphyry down at an incline of forty-five degrees. The vein held true to form, and the samples he panned each morning never failed to show a drag of gold after the concentrate. It was killing work for a man unused to pick and shovel. In the afternoon of the third day even Gary's driving energy began to slow down. He had learned how to drill and shoot in rock, but the steady swing of the four-pound hammer (miners call them single-jacks) lamed his right arm so that he could not strike a forceful blow. Moreover, he discovered that twisting a drill in rock is not soothing to broken blisters. So, much as he wanted to make Patricia rich in the shortest possible time, protesting flesh prevailed upon him to knock off work for the time being.

He was sitting on the edge of what would one day be an incline shaft—when he had dug it deep enough—inspecting his blistered hands. After several days of quiet the wind began to blow in gusts from off the butte. Somewhere behind Gary and above him there came a bellowing halloo that made him jump and slide into the open cut. Again and again came the bellow above him—and after his first astonishment Gary's mouth relaxed into a slow grin.

"I'll bet right there's the makings of that spook Voice!" he said aloud. "Up there in the rim rock somewhere."

He climbed out of the cut and stood facing the cliff, listening. At close quarters the call became a bellow with only a faint resemblance to a Voice shouting hello. He remembered now that on that first morning when he had searched for the elusive "man" on the bluff, the wind had died before he had climbed very high. After that he had not heard the Voice again that day.

He made his way laboriously up to the rim rock, listening always to locate the exact source of the sound. The bluff was almost perpendicular just under the rim, and huge bowlders lay where they had fallen in some forgotten time from the top. Gary scrambled over the first of these and confronted a narrow aperture which seemed to lead back into the cliff. The opening was perhaps three feet wide at the bottom, drawing in to a pointed roof a few feet above his head.

The Voice did not seem to come from this opening, but Gary's curiosity was roused. He went into the cave. Fifteen feet, as he paced the distance, brought him to the rear wall—and to a small recess where a couple of boxes sat side by side with a three-pound coffee can on top and a bundle wrapped in canvas. Gary forgot the Voice for the time being and began to investigate the cache.

It was perfectly simple; perfectly amazing also. The boxes had been opened, probably in order to carry the contents more easily up the bluff; the most ambitious man would scarcely want to make that climb with a fifty-pound box of dynamite on his shoulder. But both boxes were full, or so nearly full that the few missing sticks did not matter. The coffee can contained six boxes of caps, and in the canvas bundle were eight full coils of fuse.

"Golly grandma, if this ain't movie luck!" Gary jubilated to the cat, which had tagged him into the cave. "Or it would be if the dynamite were fresh. From the weird tales I've heard about men who got fresh with stale dynamite and landed in fragments before a horrified audience, Handsome Gary's liable to lose his profile if he doesn't watch his step. But it's giant powder, and if it will shoot at all, I've simply got to use it. It's just about as necessary a prop in this scene as a rope is in a lynching bee. Well, now we'll go ketchum that Voice."

By dint of hard climbing he made his way higher, to where the ledge seemed broken in splintered clefts above the slide. As he went, the Voice bellowed at him with a rising tone which distance might easily modify to a human cry. Even so close, he was some time in discovering just how the sound was made. But at last, after much listening and investigating the splintered slits, he caught the rush of wind up through a series of small, chimneylike openings. Here, then, was the Voice that had given Johnnywater Cañon so weird a reputation.

As to the appearance of the Voice just after Steve Carson's disappearance, Gary considered that an exaggeration, unconscious, perhaps, but nevertheless born of superstitious fear. Steve Carson might have told a different story could he have been questioned about the sound.

"I'd say that Injun was about due to check out, anyway," he told Faith, who was nosing a crack that probably held a rat or two. "Now I see how it's done, the Voice isn't half so mysterious or spookish as all that giant powder right on hand where I need it. Don't even have to pack it up the bluff. And that's Providence, I'll tell the cock-eyed world! When I think how I chased that supernatural Voice all over the bluff and then sat and shivered in the cabin because I couldn't find it—Faith, I should think you might have told me! You can't kid *me* into believing you weren't wise all the while. You know a heap more than you let on. You can't string *me*."

He made his way back to the cave and examined more carefully the giant powder cached there. He cut a foot length of fuse, lighted and timed it with his watch. The fuse burned with almost perfect accuracy—a minute to the foot. Then he capped a two-foot length, broke a stick of powder in two, carefully inserted the cap in the dynamite and went out and laid it under a bowlder the size of a half-barrel. He scraped loose dirt over it, split the fuse end back an inch, "spitted" it with his cigarette and ducked into the cave with his watch in his hand to await the result.

The explosion lifted the bowlder, and broke it in three pieces, and Gary felt that the experiment had been a success. The powder would probably miss fire occasionally, since it was crystallized with age. It might also explode when he least expected it to do so, but Gary was prepared to take that risk; though many an old miner would have refused profanely to touch the stuff.

"Well, I used to take a chance on breaking my neck every time I put over a stunt before the camera," he mused. "That was just to hold down a job. I ought to be dead willing to take a chance with this junk when it means millions for my girl—maybe."

With explosives enough to last him a couple of months at the very least, Gary felt that Fate was giving him a broad smile of encouragement. He acknowledged to himself, while he mortared rich pieces of porphyry and quartz that night, the growing belief that he had been all wrong in blaming Patricia for making the investment. It was, he was beginning to think, the whispering of Destiny that had urged Patricia to buy Johnnywater in the first place; and it was Destiny again at work that had pushed him out of pictures and over here to work out the plan.

Perhaps he did not reduce the thought to so definite a form, but that was the substance of his speculations.

So he dreamed and worked with untiring energy through the days, dreamed and pulped gold-bearing rock for the wedding ring during the evenings when he should have been resting, and slept like a tired baby at night. Whenever he heard the Voice shouting from the bluff, he shrugged his shoulders and grinned at the joke the wind was trying to play. Whenever he felt that unseen presence beside him, if he did not grin he at least accepted it with a certain sense of friendly companionship. And the spotted cat, Faith, was always close, like a pet dog.

CHAPTER TWENTY-FOUR
"STEVE CARSON—POOR DEVIL!"

Gary went down ten feet at an incline so sharp he could not carry the muck up in the buckets he had expected to use for the purpose. He knew, because he spent two perspiring hours in the attempt. Could he have done it, it would have been slow, toilsome work. But at least he could have gone down. He would not take the time to experiment with a ladder. To carry the necessary material up the bluff and build a thing would consume the best part of a day, and the richness of the vein bred impatience that could not brook delay.

He therefore decided to crosscut on the side where the vein showed the highest values and continue throwing out the muck. It would be slow, but Gary was thankful that he could make headway working by himself. So he drilled a round of holes in the left wall of the shaft, with the quartz and porphyry in the center of the face of the proposed crosscut. The vein on that side was wider, and the values were fully as high as on the other. He was pleased with his plan and tried to remember all he had learned about mining, so that he would waste neither time, effort, nor ore.

It takes practice to handle dynamite to the best advantage, and Gary did not always shoot the gangue cleanly away from the ore, but mixed some of his richest values with the muck. To offset that, he used the pick as much as possible and sorted the ore carefully at the bottom of the incline shaft, before he threw it to the surface.

Any experienced miner would have made better footage in a day, but it is doubtful if any man would have put in longer shifts or worked harder. And it is a great pity that Patricia could not have watched him for a day and appreciated the full strength of his devotion to her interests.

At the end of ten days, Gary had gone five feet into his crosscut, and was hoping to make better footage now that his muscles had adjusted themselves somewhat to the labor. His hands, too, had hardened amazingly. Altogether, Gary felt that he was justified in thinking mighty well of himself. There were so many things for which he was thankful, and there were so few for which he felt regret.

He did not even worry about Patricia, now that he was accomplishing something really worth while for her. It amused him to picture Patricia's astonishment when he returned to Los Angeles and told her that he had investigated Johnnywater ranch very carefully, and that she could not expect to make a nickel running cattle over there. He would tell her that his hunch had been a bird. He dramatized for himself her indignation and chuckled at the way she would fly at him for daring to convince her that she had made a foolish investment.

Then, when she had called him a lot of names and argued and squared her chin—*then* he would tell her that he had found the makings of a wedding ring at Johnnywater, and that he would expect her finger to be ready for it the minute it was cool enough to wear. After he had teased her sufficiently, he would tell her how he and the pinto cat had located "The Pat Connolly" mine; he would ask her for the job of general manager, because he would want to make sure that half of Patricia's millions were not being stolen from her.

Now that the cañon held a potential fortune, Gary could appreciate its picturesque setting and could contemplate with pleasure the prospect of spending long summers there with Patricia. He would locate sufficient claims to protect the cañon from an influx of strangers, and they would have it for their own special little corner of the world. It is astonishing how prosperity will change a man's point of view.

Six feet into the crosscut, Gary's round of holes shot unexpectedly through hard rock into a close-packed mass of broken malapi. The stuff had no logical right to be there, breaking short off the formation and vein. Had the vein pinched out and the malapi come in gradually, he might have seen some geologic reason for the change. But the whole face of his crosscut opened up malapi bowlders and "nigger-heads."

Gary filled his two buckets and carried them out into the shaft, dumping them disgustedly on the floor. It was like being shaken out of a blissful dream. He would have given a good deal just then for the presence of his old field boss, who was wise in all the vagaries of mineral formations. But there was ore still in the loosened muck, and Gary went back after it, thinking that he would make a clean job of that side before he started crosscutting the vein to the right of the shaft.

He filled one bucket. Then his shovel struck into something tough and yielding. Gary stooped, holding his candle low. He groped with his hand and pulled out a shapeless, earth-stained felt hat, with part of a skull inside it.

He dropped the gruesome thing and made for the opening, took the steep incline like a scared centipede and sat down weakly on a rock, drawing the back of his hand again and again across his clammy forehead. His knees shook. The flesh of his entire body was all aquiver with the horror of it.

Some time elapsed before Gary could even bring himself to think of the thing he had uncovered. He moved farther away, pretending that he was seeking the shade; in reality, he wanted to push a little more sunlight between the shaft and himself.

Faith came and mewed suddenly at his elbow, rubbing herself against his arm, and Gary jumped as if some one had struck him from behind. The contact of the cat set him quivering again, and he pushed her away from him with a backward sweep of his arm. Faith retreated to another rock and stood there with her back arched, regarding him fixedly in round-eyed amazement. Gary slid off the bowlder and started down the bluff, his going savoring strongly of retreat. He was not particularly squeamish, nor had he ever been called a coward; nevertheless the grisly discovery drove him from the spot with the very unexpectedness of the disinterment.

At the cabin he stopped and looked back up the bluff, ashamed of his flight.

"Steve Carson—the poor devil!" he muttered under his breath. "A cave-in caught him, I reckon. And nobody ever knew what became of him."

He walked aimlessly to the corral, perhaps seeking the small comfort of even the horse's presence. He gave Jazz an extra forkful of hay and stood leaning his elbows upon the top rail of the corral, watching Jazz nose the heap for the tenderest morsels. The phlegmatic content of the old horse steadied him. He could think of the horror now, without shaking inside like joggled jelly.

He looked at his watch and saw that it lacked half an hour until noon. There would be time enough to do what he knew must be done, if he were to have any future peace in Johnnywater Cañon.

He found an extra pick, shouldered the long-handled irrigating shovel and set out to find a suitable spot—not too close to the house—where he might give the shattered bones of Steve Carson decent burial. He chose the tiny knoll crowned with the thick-branched juniper and dug the grave there that afternoon. For the time being he must leave the body where it was, crushed under the cave-in.

"But he stayed there for five years," Gary excused the seeming slight. "One more night shouldn't hurt him."

It was an uncomfortable night, however, for Gary. Even in his sleep the thought of that broken body would not leave him. It overshadowed all his hopes and dreams, and even Patricia seemed very far away, and life seemed very short and uncertain.

The next day Gary devoted to moving what little was left of Steve Carson from under the mass of broken rock and burying the remains in the grave under the juniper. The mottled cat walked solemnly behind him all the way; and it seemed to Gary that the unseen yet sentient spirit of the man walked beside him.

CHAPTER TWENTY-FIVE
THE VALUE OF A HUNCH

The resiliency of youth, aided by the allurement of riches to be gained by digging, drove Gary back up the bluff to his work. Here again circumstances had forced him to continue where he would voluntarily have left off. In digging out the body of Steve Carson, Gary had dug completely through the broken stuff to a continuation of the vein and its contact beyond.

He felt that he understood in a general way what had happened five years ago. Steve Carson had undoubtedly discovered the gold-bearing quartz and had started to sink on the vein much as Gary had done. The calamity of a cave-in—or perhaps a slide—had overtaken him while he was at work underground. He had never known what hit him, which was a mercy. And since no one in the country had heard of the prospect up on the bluff, the discovery of his body would never have been made if Gary had not followed the cat up there and so stumbled upon the vein.

He thought he also understood now why Faith had shown her strange penchant for that particular spot on the bluff. Monty had told him that the cat had belonged to Steve Carson. She had undoubtedly been in the habit of following Steve Carson to work, just as she followed Gary. Very likely she had been somewhere near at the time when her master was killed. That she should continue the habit of going each day to the spot where she had last seen him was not unlikely. So another small mystery was cleared to Gary's satisfaction. Save for its grim history, Johnnywater Cañon was likely to drop at last to the dead level of commonplace respectability.

If Steve Carson had worked in an open shaft that had been filled by a slide, the opening had been effectually blocked afterward. For on the surface Gary could see no evidence whatever, among the piled bowlders, of an opening beneath. And the roof, when he lifted his candle to examine it, looked to be a smooth expanse of rock.

For himself, he pronounced his own incline shaft safe from any similar catastrophe. He had started it at the extreme edge of the slide, and above it the rocks seemed firmly in place. He was working under dangerous conditions, it is true; but the danger lay in using five-year-old dynamite. Still, he must chance it or let the development of Patricia's claim stand still.

Pondering the necessary steps to protect Patricia in case anything happened to him, Gary wrote a copy of his location notice, declared the necessary location work done, described the exact spot as closely as possible—lining it up with blazed trees in the grove behind the cabin, and placed the papers in his suit case. That, he knew, would effectually forestall any claim-jumping;

unless James Blaine Hawkins or some other crook appeared first on the scene and ransacked his belongings, destroying the papers and placing their own location notices on the claim. He felt that the danger of such villainy was slight and not worth considering seriously. Monty would probably ride over as soon as he had finished his work in Pahranagat Valley; and when he did, Gary meant to tell him all about it and take him up and show him the claim.

Monty would keep the secret for him, he was sure. He did not want Patricia to know anything about it until he was sure that the vein was not going to peter out before it yielded at least a modest fortune.

One night soon after he had made these elaborate arrangements, Gary woke sweating from a nightmare. He was so sure that James Blaine Hawkins was rummaging through his suit case, looking for the information of the mine, that he swung out of bed, kicking viciously with both feet. When they failed to land upon the man he believed was there, Gary drew back and kicked again at a different angle.

Not a sound save Gary's breathing disturbed the midnight quiet of the cabin. Gary waited, wondering foolishly if he had been dreaming after all. He leaned and reached for his trousers, found a match and lighted it. The tiny blaze flared up and showed him an empty cabin. It was a dream, then—but a disagreeably vivid one, that impressed upon Gary's mind the thought that James Blaine Hawkins, returning while he was at work up the bluff, would be very likely to go prowling. If he found and read Gary's explicit description of the mine and the way to find it, together with his opinion of its richness, James Blaine Hawkins might be tempted to slip up there and roll a rock down on Gary.

Wherefore, Gary dragged his suit case from under the bed, found the papers, lighted another match and burned them. When that was done to his satisfaction, he lay down again and went to sleep. Books might be written—and possibly have been—about hunches, their origin and value, if any. Gary's nightmare and the strong impulse afterward to guard against danger, took a wrong turning somewhere. He provided against a danger which did not exist in reality and felt an instant relief. And soon after sunrise he shouldered a full canteen, stuffed a five-pound lard bucket as full of lunch as he could cram it, got a handful of fresh candles and went blithely up the bluff to meet the greatest danger that had ever threatened him in his life.

He had driven the crosscut in a good twelve feet by now, and he was proud of his work. The vein seemed to be widening a bit, and the values still held. Already he had an ore dump which he estimated should bring Patricia almost as much money as she had paid for Johnnywater. He hoped there was more than that in the dump, but he was clinging to the side of conservatism. If the claim yielded no more than that, he could still feel that he had done Patricia a real service. To-day he carried his gold dust knotted in a handkerchief in his pocket, lest his nightmare should come true and James Blaine Hawkins should return to rob him. He even carried the mortar and pestle to the shed and threw them down in a corner with the gold pan tucked under some steel traps, so that no one could possibly suspect that they had been used lately.

He was thinking of James Blaine Hawkins while he drilled the four holes in the face of the crosscut. He stopped to listen and looked down the cañon and out as far as he could see into the desert when he went up into the hot sunlight to get the powder, fuse and caps from the cave to load the holes. As he sat in the shade crimping the caps on the four lengths of fuse, a vague uneasiness grew upon him.

"I got a hunch he'll turn up to-day—and maybe bring some strong-arm guy with him," Gary said to himself. "Just so he doesn't happen along in time to hear the shots up here, I don't know what harm he could do. He never could find this place, even if he got some hint there was a mine somewhere. Anyway, I could hear him drive up the cañon, all right."

Still he was charging his mental disturbance to James Blaine Hawkins— which proves how inaccurate a "hunch" may be. He carried his four loads to the incline shaft and let himself carefully down, the explosive cuddled in one arm while he steadied himself with the other. At the bottom he noticed his second canteen lying in the full glare of the sun and moved it inside the crosscut with the other canteen and his lunch. It was an absent-minded act, since he would presently move everything outside clear of flung rocks from the blasting.

Still fighting the vague depression that seemed the aftermath of his nightmare, Gary loaded the holes with more care than usual, remembering that he was playing with death whenever he handled that old powder. He flung shovel and pick toward the opening, split the fuse ends with his knife and turned to hurry out of the shaft.

He faced the opening just in time to see it close as a great bowlder dropped into the shaft, followed by the clatter of smaller rocks.

Instinctively Gary recoiled and got the smell of the burning fuse in his nostrils. Without conscious thought of what he must do, he whipped out his knife, tore open a blade and cut the fuses, one by one, close to the rock. He stamped upon them—though they were harmless, writhing there on the floor of the crosscut until the powder was exhausted.

Not until the last fuse stopped burning did Gary approach the blocked opening to see how badly he was trapped. A little rift of sunlight showed at the upper right-hand corner. The rest was black, solid rock. Gary felt the rock all over with his hands, then stooped and lifted his lunch and the two canteens and set them farther back in the crosscut, as if he feared they might yet be destroyed.

He moved the candle here and there above the floor, looking desperately for his pick and shovel. But the heave he had given them had sent them out into the shaft directly in the path of the falling bowlder. He searched the crosscut for other tools, and found his single-jack leaning against the wall where he had dropped it; beside it were two of the shorter drills, the bits nicked and dull.

He returned to the closed mouth of the crosscut and attempted to pry away the bowlder, using the longer of the two drills thrust into the opening as a lever. He could as easily have tilted the rim rock itself. Sunlight streamed in through a crack possibly eighteen inches long and the width of his hand, but except for the ventilation it gave, the opening merely served to emphasize the hopelessness of his prison.

He looked at his watch mechanically, and saw that it was just fifteen minutes past twelve. He had timed his work, like all good miners, so that he could "shoot" at noon and let the smoke clear away from the workings while he rested and ate his lunch. He did not feel like eating now. He did not feel like much of anything. His brain refused to react immediately to the full horror of his position.

That he, Gary Marshall, should actually be entombed alive in Patricia's gold mine—"The Pat Connolly" mine—was a thing too incredible for his mind to grasp. He simply could not take the thing seriously.

The unreasoning belief that Mills would presently shout, "Cut!" and Gary would walk out into the sunlight, persisted for a time. The dramatic element loomed high above the grim reality of it. The thing was too ghastly to be true. To believe in the horrible truth of it would drive a man crazy, he told himself impatiently.

He put his face to the widest part of the opening between the bowlder and the wall, and shouted again and again frenziedly.

"*Monty! Oh-h, Monty!*" he called.

The pity of it was that Monty Girard was at that moment jogging into the mouth of Johnnywater Cañon, swinging his feet boyishly in the stirrups and humming a little song as he rode, his thoughts with Gary, wondering how he was "making it" these days.

CHAPTER TWENTY-SIX
"GARY MARSHALL MYSTERIOUSLY MISSING"

By riding as late as he dared that night, and letting the horses rest until daylight the next morning, and then pushing them forward at top desert speed—which was a steady trail trot—Monty reached the first ranch house a little after noon the next day. In all that time he had not seen a human being, though he had hoped to be overtaken or to meet some car on the road.

Nerve-racking delay met him at the ranch. The woman and two small children were there, but the man (Ben Thompson was his name) had left that morning for Las Vegas in the car. Monty was too late by about four hours.

He ate dinner there, fed his horses hay and grain, watered them the last minute and started out again, still hoping that some car would be traveling that way. But luck was against him and he was forced to camp that night thirty miles out from Las Vegas.

Long before daylight he was up and on his way again, to take advantage of the few hours before the intense heat of the day began. Jazz was going lame, traveling barefooted at the forced pace Monty required of him. It was nearly five o'clock when he limped into town with the dusty pack roped upon his sweat-encrusted back.

Monty went directly to the depot and climbed the steep stairs to the telegraph office, his spur rowels burring along the boards. He leaned heavily upon the shelf outside the grated window while he wrote two messages with a hand that shook from exhaustion.

The first was addressed to the sheriff of Nye County, notifying him that a man had disappeared in Johnnywater Cañon and that it looked like murder. The other read as follows:

"P. Connolly,
Cons. Grain & Milling Co.,
Los Angeles, Calif.

"Gary Marshall mysteriously missing from Johnnywater evidence points to foul play suspect Hawkins wire instructions.

"M. Girard."

Monty regretted the probable shock that message would give to Patricia, but he reasoned desperately that she would have to know the worst anyway, and that a telegram never permits much softening of a blow. She might know something about Hawkins that would be helpful. At any rate, he knew of no one so intimately concerned as Patricia.

He waited for his change, asked the operator to rush both messages straight through, and clumped heavily down the stairs. He remounted and made straight for the nearest stable and turned the horses over to the proprietor himself, who he knew would give them the best care possible. After that he went to a hotel, got a room with bath, took a cold plunge and crawled between the hot sheets with the window as wide open as it would go, and dropped immediately into the heavy slumber of complete mental and physical exhaustion.

While Monty was refreshing himself with the cold bath, Gary, squatted on his heels against the wall of his dungeon, was fingering half of a hoarded biscuit and trying to decide whether he had better eat it now and turn a bold face toward starvation, or put it back in the lard bucket and let the thought of it torture him for a few more hours.

The telegram to the sheriff at Tonopah arrived while the sheriff was hunting down a murderer elsewhere. His deputy read the wire and speared it face down upon a bill-hook already half filled with a conglomerate mass of other communications. The deputy was not inclined to attach much significance to the message. He frequently remarked that if the sheriff's office got all fussed up over every yarn that came in, the county would be broke inside a month paying mileage and salary to a dozen deputies. Monty had not said that a man had been murdered. He merely suspected something of the sort. The deputy slid down deeper into the armchair he liked best, cocked his feet higher on the desk and filled his pipe. Johnnywater Cañon and the possible fate of the man who had disappeared from there entered not at all into his somnolent meditations.

The telegram to Patricia reached the main office in Los Angeles after five o'clock. The clerk who telephones the messages called up the office of the Consolidated Grain & Milling Company and got no reply after repeated ringing. Patricia's telegram was therefore held until office hours the next morning. A messenger boy delivered it last, on his first trip out that way with half-a-dozen messages. The new stenographer was not at first inclined to take it, thinking there must be some mistake. The new manager was in conference with an important customer and she was afraid to disturb him with a matter so unimportant. And since she had quarreled furiously with the bookkeeper just the day before, she would not have spoken to him for anything on earth. So Patricia's telegram lay on the desk until nearly noon.

At last the manager happened to stroll into the outer office and picked up the yellow envelope which had not been opened. Being half in love with Patricia—in spite of a wife—he knew at once who "P. Connolly" was. He was a conscientious man though his affections did now and then stray from his own hearthside. He immediately called a messenger and sent the telegram back to the main office with forwarding instructions.

At that time, Gary was standing before the sunny slit at the end of the crosscut, pounding doggedly with the single-jack at the corner of the rock wall. He had given up attempting to use the dulled drill as a gadget. He could no longer strike with sufficient force to make the steel bite into the rock, nor could he land the blow accurately on the head of the drill.

The day before he had managed to crack off a piece of rock twice the width of his hand; and though it had broken too far inside the crosscut to accomplish much in the way of enlarging the opening, Gary was nevertheless vastly encouraged. He could now thrust out his hand to the elbow. He could feel the sun shine hot upon it at midday. He could feel the warm wind in his face when he held it pressed close against the open space. He could even smooth Faith's sleek head when she scrambled upon the bowlder and peered in at him round-eyed and anxious. The world that day had seemed very close.

But to-day, while the telegram to Patricia was loitering in Los Angeles, the sky over Johnnywater was filled thick with clouds. Daylight came gray into the deep gloom of the crosscut. And Gary could not swing a steady blow, but pounded doggedly at the rock with quick, short-arm strokes like a woodpecker hammering at the bole of a dead tree.

He was obliged to stop often and rest, leaning against the wall with his hunger-sharpened profile like a cameo where the light shone in upon him. He would stand there and pant for a while and then lift the four-pound hammer—grown terribly heavy, lately—and go on pounding unavailingly at the rock.

CHAPTER TWENTY-SEVEN
"NOBODY KNOWS BUT A PINTO CAT"

Patricia liked Kansas City even less than she had anticipated. She dragged herself through the heat to the office each morning, worried somehow through her work and returned to her room too utterly depressed and weary to seek what enjoyment lay close at hand. A little park was just across the street, but Patricia could not even summon sufficient interest to enter it. Every cloud that rose over the horizon was to her imagination a potential cyclone, which she rather hoped would sweep her away. She thought she would like to be swept into a new world; and if she could leave her memory behind her she thought that life might be almost bearable.

No mail had been forwarded to her from Los Angeles, and the utter silence served to deepen her general pessimism. And then, an hour before closing time on the hottest day she had ever experienced in her life, here came the telegram for P. Connolly.

"Gary Marshall mysteriously missing from Johnnywater———" Patricia blinked and read again incredulously. The remainder of the message, "evidence points to foul play suspect Hawkins wire instructions" sounded to her suspiciously like one of Gary's jokes. She was obliged to read the signature, "M. Girard," over several times, and to make sure that it was sent from Las Vegas, Nevada, before she could even begin to accept the message as authentic.

How in the world could Gary be mysteriously missing from Johnnywater when he had flatly refused to go there? How could Hawkins be suspected? P. Connolly went suddenly into a white, wilted heap in her chair.

When she opened her eyes the assistant bookkeeper was standing over her with a glass of water, and her boss was hurrying in from his office. Some one had evidently called him. Her boss was not the kind of man who wastes time on nonessentials. He did not ask Patricia if she were ill or what was the matter. He picked up the open telegram and read it with one long, comprehensive glance. Then he placed his hand under Patricia's arm, told her that she was all right, that the heat did those things in Kansas City, and added the information that there was a breeze blowing in the corner window of his office. Patricia suffered him to lead her away from the gaping office force.

"Sit right there until you feel better," her boss commanded, pushing her rather gently into a chair in the coolest corner of the room.

"I feel better now," Patricia told him gamely. "I received a telegram that knocked me over for a minute. I didn't know what it meant. If you don't mind, Mr. Wilson, I should like to go and attend to the matter."

Mr. Wilson handed her the telegram with a dry smile. "It sounds rather ominous, I admit," he observed, omitting an apology for having read it. "Naturally I cannot advise you, since I do not understand what it is all about. But if you wish to wire any instructions, just write your message here while I call the messenger. There was a delay, remember. The message was forwarded from Los Angeles."

"Thank you, Mr. Wilson," Patricia answered in her prim office tone. "I should like to reply at once, if you don't mind. And, Mr. Wilson, if you will be so good as to O. K. a check for me, I shall take the next train to Las Vegas, Nevada."

"I'll 'phone for a ticket and reservations," her boss announced without hesitation. "You will want to be sure of having enough money to see you through, of course. I can arrange an advance on your salary, if you wish."

Patricia told him, in not quite so prim a tone, that it would not be necessary. She wrote her message asking Monty Girard to wait until she arrived, as she was taking the next train. The messenger, warned by a certain look in the eye of the boss, ducked his head and departed almost running. Patricia wrote her check and the boss sent it to the cashier by the office boy; and telephoned the ticket office. Patricia read the telegram again very slowly.

"Johnnywater is the name of a cattle ranch which I happen to own in Nevada, Mr. Wilson," Patricia said in the steadiest voice she could command. "Hawkins is a man I sent over to take charge of the ranch and run it on shares. You'll see why I must go and look into this matter." You will observe that Patricia, having come up gasping for breath, was still saying, "Scissors!" with secret relish.

Even in her confused state of apprehension, there was a certain gratification to Patricia in seeing that the boss was impressed by the fact that she owned a cattle ranch in Nevada. She was also glad that it had not been necessary to explain the identity of Gary Marshall. But immediately it became necessary.

"This Gary Marshall who disappeared; do you know him?"

"I'm engaged to marry him," Patricia replied in as neutral a tone as she could manage. "I didn't know he was at Johnnywater," she added truthfully. "That's why I thought it was a joke when I first read it. I still don't understand how he could be there at all. He was playing the lead in a picture when I left Los Angeles."

"You don't mean Gary Marshall, the Western star?" The boss's tone was distinctly exclamatory. Patricia saw that her engagement to Gary Marshall impressed the boss much more deeply than did her ownership of Johnnywater ranch. "That young man is going right to the top in pictures. He acts with his brains and forgets his good looks. Most of 'em do it the other way round. Why, I'd rather go and see Gary Marshall in a picture than any star I know! And you're engaged to him! Well, well! I didn't know, Miss Connolly, that I was so closely related to my favorite movie star. May I see that telegram again? Lord, I'd hate to think anything'd happened to that boy—but don't you worry! If I'm not mistaken, he's a lad that can take care of himself where most men would go under. By all means, go and see what's wrong. And I wish, Miss Connolly, you'd wire me as soon as you find that everything is all right. You *will* find it all right—I'm absolutely positive on that point."

Patricia cherished a deep respect for her boss. She felt suddenly convicted of a great wrong. She had never dreamed that a man with the keen, analytical mind of John S. Wilson could actually respect a fellow who worked in the movies. She left the office humbled and anxious to make amends.

That evening the boss himself took her to the train and saw that she was comfortable, and spoke encouragingly of Gary's ability to take care of himself, no matter what danger threatened. His encouragement, however, only served to alarm Patricia the more. She was a shrewd young woman, and she read deep concern in the mind of her boss, from the very fact that he had taken the pains to reassure her.

That night Gary dreamed that Steve Carson stood suddenly before him and spoke to him. He dreamed that Steve Carson told him he would not starve to death in there, for his sweetheart was coming with men who would dig him out.

Gary woke with the dream so vivid in his mind that he could scarcely reason himself out of the belief that Steve Carson had actually talked with him. Gary lay thinking of Sir Ernest Shackleton, of whose voyages to the Antarctic he had read again and again. He recalled how close Shackleton and his companions had shaved starvation, not from necessity, but from choice, in the interests of science. He tried to guess what Shackleton would do, were he in Gary's predicament, with four candles and the stub of a fifth in his possession, and approximately two gallons of water.

"I bet he'd go strong for several days yet," Gary whispered. "He'd cut the candles into little bits and eat one piece and call it a meal. And he'd figure out just how many wallops he could give that damned rock on the strength of his gorgeous feed of one inch of candle. And then, when he'd dined on the last wick and hit the rock a last wallop, he'd grin and say it had been a great game." He turned painfully over upon the other side and laid his face upon his bent arm.

"Shackleton never was shut up in a hole a hundred miles from nowhere," he murmured, "with nobody knowing a word about it but a pinto cat that's crazy over spiritualism. If Shackleton was here, I bet he'd say, 'Eat the candles, boy, and take your indigestion all at one time and finish the game.' No use dragging out the suspense till the audience gets the gapes. First time I ever starred in a story that had an unhappy ending. I didn't think the Big Director would do it!"

He lay for a time dozing and trying to forget the terrible gnawing in his stomach. Then his thoughts wandered on and he mumbled,

"I'm not kicking—if this is the way it's supposed to be. But I did want Pat to have her gold mine. And now the location work is all covered up—so maybe it won't count. And some other gink will maybe come along and jump the claim, and my Pat won't get her gold mine. I guess it's all right. But I didn't think the Big Director would do this!"

CHAPTER TWENTY-EIGHT
MONTY MEETS PATRICIA

Monty had made up his mind to go on to Los Angeles and see for himself why Patricia would not answer his telegram, when he received the word that she was coming from Kansas City. He swore a good deal over the delay that would hold him inactive in town. To fill in the time he wrote a long letter to the sheriff in Tonopah, stating all the facts in the case so far as he knew them. He hoped that the sheriff was already on his way to Johnnywater, though Monty could not have told just what he expected the sheriff to accomplish when he arrived there.

He tried to trace James Blaine Hawkins, but only succeeded in learning from a garage man that Hawkins had come in off the desert at least three weeks before, cursed the roads and the country in general and had left for Los Angeles. Or at least that was the destination he had named.

Even Monty could find no evidence in that of Hawkins' guilt. His restless pacing up and down the three short blocks that comprised the main business street of the town got on the nerves of the men who knew him. His concern over Gary Marshall gradually infected the minds of others; so that news of a murder committed in Johnnywater Cañon was wired to the city papers, and the Chief of Police in Los Angeles was advised also by wire to trace James Blaine Hawkins if possible.

Old cuts of Gary Marshall were hastily dug up in newspaper offices and his picture run on the first page. A reporter who knew him well wrote a particularly dramatic special article, which was copied more or less badly by many of the papers. Cohen got to hear of it, and his publicity agents played up the story magnificently, not because Cohen wished to immortalize one of his younger leading men who was out of the game, but because it made splendid indirect advertising for Cohen.

Monty, of course, never dreamed that he had done all this. He was sincerely grieving over Gary, whose grave he thought he had discovered by the bushy juniper. The mere fact that James Blaine Hawkins had appeared in Las Vegas approximately three weeks before did not convince him that Gary had not been murdered. He believed that Hawkins had lain in wait for Gary and had killed him on his return from Kawich. The grave might easily be that old.

Of course there was a weak point in that argument. In fact, Monty's state of mind was such that he failed to see the fatally weak point until the day of Patricia's arrival. When he did see it he abandoned the theory in disgust, threw out his hands expressively, and declared that he didn't give a damn just how the crime had been committed, or when. Without a doubt his friend,

Gary Marshall, had been killed, and Monty swore he would never rest until the murderer had paid the price. The weak point, which was the well-fed comfort of the pigs and Jazz, he did not attempt to explain away. Perhaps James Blaine Hawkins had not gone to Los Angeles at all. Perhaps he was still out there at Johnnywater, and Monty had failed to discover him.

He was in that frame of mind when he met the six o'clock train that brought Patricia. Naturally, he had no means of identifying her. But he followed a tired-looking girl with a small black handbag to one of the hotels and inspected the register just as she turned away from the desk. Then he took off his hat, extended his hand and told her who he was.

Patricia was all for starting for Johnnywater that night. Monty gave her one long look and told her bluntly that it simply couldn't be done; that no one could travel the road at night. His eyes were very blue and convincing, and his southern drawl branded the lie as truth. Wherefore, Patricia rested that night in a bed that remained stationary, and by morning Monty was better satisfied with her appearance and believed that she would stand the trip all right.

"I reckon maybe yuh-all better find some woman to go on out, Miss Connolly," Monty suggested while they breakfasted.

"I can't see why that should be necessary, Mr. Girard," Patricia replied in her primmest office tone. "I am perfectly able to take care of myself, I should think."

"You'll be the only woman in the country for about sixty-five or seventy miles," Monty warned her diffidently. "Uh course there couldn't anything happen to yuh-all—but I expect the sheriff and maybe one or two more will be down from Tonopah when we get there, and I thought maybe yuh-all might like to have some other woman along for company."

He dipped three spoons of sugar into his coffee and looked at Patricia with a sympathetic look in his eyes.

"I was thinkin' last night, Miss Connolly, that I dunno as there's much use of your going out there at all. Yuh-all couldn't do a thing, and it's liable to be mighty unpleasant. When I sent that wire to yuh-all, I never thought a word about yuh-all comin' to Johnnywater. What I wanted was to get a line on this man, Hawkins. I thought maybe yuh-all could tell me something about him."

Patricia glanced unseeingly around the insufferably hot little café. She was not conscious of the room at all. She was thinking of Gary and trying to force herself to a calmness that could speak of him without betraying her feelings.

"I don't know anything about Mr. Hawkins, other than that I arranged with him to run the ranch on shares," she said, and the effort she was making made her voice sound very cold and impersonal. "I certainly did not know that Mr. Marshall was at Johnnywater, or I should not have sent Mr. Hawkins over. I had asked Mr. Marshall first to take charge of the ranch, and Mr. Marshall had refused, on the ground that he did not wish to give up his work in motion pictures. Are you sure that he came over here and was at Johnnywater when Mr. Hawkins arrived?" Patricia did not know it, but her voice sounded as coldly accusing as if she were a prosecuting attorney trying to make a prisoner give damaging testimony against himself. Her manner bred a slight resentment in Monty, so that he forgot his diffidence.

"I hauled Gary Marshall out to Johnnywater myself, over six weeks ago," he told her bluntly. "He hunted me up and acted like he wanted to scrap with me because he thought I'd helped to cheat yuh-all. He was going to sell the place for yuh-all if he could—and I sure approved of the idea. It ain't any place for a lady to own. A man could go there and live like a hermit and make a bare living, but yuh-all couldn't divide the profits and break even. I dunno as there'd *be* any profits to divide, after a feller'd paid for his grub and clothes.

"Gary saw it right away, and I was to bring him back to town in a couple of days; but I had an accident to my car so I couldn't come in. I reckon Gary meant to write anyway and tell yuh-all where he was. But he never had a chance to send out a letter."

Patricia dipped a spoon into her cereal and left it there. "Even so, I don't believe Gary disappeared very mysteriously," she said, her chin squaring itself. "He probably got tired of staying there and went back to Los Angeles by way of Tonopah. However, I shall drive out and see the ranch, now that I'm here. I'm very sorry you have been put to so much trouble, Mr. Girard. I really think Mr. Marshall should have left some word for you before he left. But then," she added with some bitterness, "he didn't seem to think it necessary to let *me* know he was coming over here. And we have telephones in Los Angeles, Mr. Girard."

Monty's eyes were very blue and steady when he looked at her across the table. He set down his cup and leaned forward a little.

"If yuh spoke to Gary in that tone of voice, Miss Connolly," he drawled, "I reckon he wouldn't feel much like usin' the telephone before he left town. Gary's as nice a boy as I ever met in my life."

Patricia bit her under lip, and a tinge of red crept up over her cheek bones to the dark circles beneath her eyes, that told a tale of sleepless nights which Patricia herself would have denied.

The remainder of the breakfast was a silent meal, with only such speech as was necessary and pertained to the trip before them. Monty advised the taking out of certain supplies and assisted Patricia in making up a list of common comforts which could be carried in a touring car.

He left her at the hotel while he attended to the details of getting under way, and when he returned it was with a Ford and driver, and many parcels stacked in the tonneau. Patricia's suit case was wedged between the front fender and the tucked-up hood of the motor, and a bundle of new bedding was jammed down upon the other side in like manner. Patricia herself was wedged into the rear seat beside the parcels and packages of food. Her black traveling bag Monty deposited between his feet in front with the driver.

At the last moment, while the driver was cranking the motor, Monty reached backward with a small package in his hand.

"Put on these sun goggles," he said. "Your eyes will be a fright if you ride all day against this wind without any protection."

"Thank you very much, Mr. Girard," said Patricia with a surprising meekness— for her. What is more, she put on the hideous amber glasses; though she hated the jaundiced look they gave to the world.

Patricia had a good deal to think about during that interminable, jolting ride. She was given ample opportunity for the thinking, since Monty Girard never spoke to her except to inquire now and then if she were comfortable.

CHAPTER TWENTY-NINE
GARY ROBS THE PINTO CAT OF HER DINNER

That same morning Gary finished his third candle and tried his best to make one swallow of water, held long in his parched mouth, suffice for two hours.

He could no longer lift the single-jack to the height of his shoulder, much less strike a blow upon the rock. He leaned against the bowlder and struck a few feeble blows with the head of the longer of the two drills; but the steel bounced back futilely, and the exertion tired him so that he was forced to desist after a few minutes of heart-breaking effort.

He sat down with his back against the wall where the sunlight could find him and give a little cheer to his prison, and fingered his fourth candle longingly. He licked his cracked lips and lifted the canteen, his emaciated fingers fumbling the screw-top thirstily. He tried to reason sensibly with himself that only a cowardly reluctance to meet death—which was the inevitable goal of life—held him fighting there in that narrow dungeon, scheming to add a few more tortured hours to his life.

He told himself angrily that he was merely holding up the action of the story, and that the scene should be cut right there. In other words, there was absolutely no hope of his ever getting out of there, alive or dead. Steve Carson, he mumbled, had been lucky. He had at least taken his exit quickly.

"But I ain't licked yet," he croaked, with a cracked laugh. "There's a lot of fight in me yet. Never had any use for a quitter. Steve Carson wouldn't have quit—only he got beaned with the first rock and couldn't fight. I'm not hurt—yet. Trained down pretty fine, is all. When I'm a ghost, maybe I'll come back and tell fat ladies with Ouija boards in their laps how to reduce. Great scheme. I'll do that little thing. But I ain't whipped yet—not until I've tried out my jackknife on that damned rock. Have a drink, old son. And then get to work! What the hell are you loafing for?"

He lifted the lightened canteen, his arms shaking with weakness, and took another drink of water. Then, carefully screwing on the top of the canteen, he set it down gently against the wall and reached wearily into his pocket. The blade of his knife had never been so hard to open; but he accomplished it and pulled himself laboriously to his feet. Steadying himself with one hand against the malapi bowlder that shut him in, he went to the opening—widened now so that he could thrust forth his arm to the shoulder—and began carefully chipping at a seam in the rock with the largest blade of his jackknife.

He really did not expect to free himself by that means; nor by any other. Since he began to weaken he had come to accept his fate with such calmness as his pride in playing the game could muster. But he could not sit idle and wait for death to creep upon him. Nor could he hurry it, which he held to be a coward's trick. He still believed that the "Big Director" should be obeyed. It was too late now to ask for another part in the picture. He had been cast for this rôle and he would play it to the final scene.

So he stood hacking and prying with his knife blade, stopping now and then to stare out into the hot sunshine. He could even see a wisp of cloud drift across the bit of blue sky revealed to him through the narrow rock window of his prison. The sight made him grit his teeth. He was so close to that free, sun-drenched world, and he was yet so utterly helpless!

He was standing so, resting from his unavailing task, when the spotted cat hopped upon the bowlder where every day she sat to be stroked by Gary's hand. Gary's eyes narrowed and he licked his lips avidly. Faith was carrying a wild dove that she had caught and brought to the bowlder where she might feast in pleasant company.

"Thanks, old girl," he said grimly; and stretching out his arm, snatched the bird greedily from Faith's mouth. "Some service! Now beat it and go catch a rabbit; a big one. Catch two rabbits!"

He slid down to a sitting position and began plucking the limp body of the dove, his fingers trembling with eagerness. The "third hunger" was upon him—that torment of craving which men who have been entombed in mines speak of with lowered voices—if they live to tell about it. Gary longed to tear the bird with his teeth, just as it was.

But he would not yield an inch from his idea of the proper way to play the game. He therefore plucked the dove almost clean of feathers, and lighting his one precious remaining candle, he turned the small, plump body over the candle flame, singeing it before he held the flame to its breast.

The instant that portion was seared and partially broiled, Gary set his handsome white teeth into it and chewed the morsel slowly while he broiled another bite. His impulse—rather, the agonized craving of his whole famished body—was to tear the body asunder with his teeth and devour it like an animal. But he steeled himself to self-control; just as he had held himself sternly in hand down in the cabin when loneliness and that weird, felt presence plucked at his courage.

He would have grudged the melting of even the half-inch of tallow it required to broil the bird so that he could eat it and retain his self-respect; but the succulent flesh was too delicious. He could not think of anything but the ecstasy of eating.

He crunched the bones in his teeth, pulping them slowly, extracting the last particle of flavor and nourishment. When he had finished there remained but the head and the feet—and he flung them through the opening lest he should be tempted to devour them also. After that he indulged himself in a sip of water, stretched himself full length upon the rock floor, and descended blissfully into the oblivion of deep slumber.

CHAPTER THIRTY
"SOMEBODY HOLLERED UP ON THE BLUFF"

The left front tire of the town Ford persisted in going flat with a slow valve leak. The driver, a heedless young fellow, had neglected to bring extra valves; so that the tire needed pumping every ten miles or such a matter. Then the Ford began heating on the long, uphill pull between the Pintwater Mountains and the Spotted Range, and some time was lost during the heat of the day because of the necessity for cooling the motor. Delays such as these eat away the hours on a long trip; wherefore it was nearly dusk when Patricia got her first glimpse of Johnnywater Cañon.

Up in the crosscut, Gary heard the rumbling throb of the motor, and shouted until he was exhausted. Which did not take long, even with the nourishment of the broiled dove to refresh his failing strength.

He consoled himself afterward with the thought that it was James Blaine Hawkins come sneaking back, and that he would like nothing better than to find Gary hopelessly caged in the crosscut. Gary was rather glad that James Blaine Hawkins had failed to hear him shout. At any rate, the secret of Patricia's mine was safe from him, and Gary would be spared the misery of being taunted by Hawkins. It was a crazy notion, for it was not at all likely that even James Blaine Hawkins would have let him die so grisly a death. But Gary was harboring strange notions at times during the last forty-eight hours. And the body of one wild dove was pitifully inadequate for the needs of a starving man.

Monty had not meant to be cruel. Now that he was on the spot, he tried his best to soften the shock of what he knew Patricia must discover. That morning he had purposely avoided speaking of his reasons for fearing the worst. Then Patricia's manner—assumed merely to hide her real emotion—had chilled Monty to silence on the whole subject. With the driver present they had not discussed the matter at all during the trip, so that Patricia was still ignorant of what Monty believed to be the real, tragic state of affairs.

Monty looked up from lighting a fire in the stove and saw Patricia go over to Gary's coat and smooth it caressingly with her hand. Then and there he forgave Patricia for her tone at breakfast. She took Gary's hat from the cupboard and held it in her hands, her eyes questioning Monty.

"Gary was saving that hat till he went to town again," Monty informed her in his gentle drawl. "He was wearing an old hat of Waddell's, and some old clothes Waddell left here when he pulled out. You see now, Miss Connolly, one reason why I don't believe Gary went to Tonopah. His suit case is there, too, under the bunk. But don't yuh-all worry—we'll find him."

He turned back to his fire-building, and Patricia sat down on the edge of the bunk and stared wide-eyed around the cabin.

So this was why she had failed to hear from Gary in all these weeks! He had come over here to Johnnywater after all, because she wished it. She had never dreamed the place would be so lonely. And Gary had lived here all alone!

"Is this all there is to the house—just this one room?" she asked Monty abruptly, in her prim, colorless tone.

"Yes, ma'am, this is the size of it," Monty replied cheerfully. "Folks don't generally waste much time on buildin' fancy houses, out here. Most generally they're mighty thankful if the walls keep out the wind and the roof don't leak. If it's dry and warm, they don't care if it ain't stylish."

"Is this the way Gary left it?" she asked next, glancing down at the rough board floor that gave evidence of having been lately scrubbed.

"Yes, ma'am, except for the dust on things. Gary Marshall was a right neat housekeeper, Miss Connolly."

"*Was?*" Patricia stood up and came toward him. "Do you think he's—what makes you say *was?*"

Monty hedged. "Well, he ain't been keepin' house here for a week, anyway. It's a week ago yesterday I rode over here from my camp. Things are just as they was then."

"You have something else on your mind, Mr. Girard. What was it that made you wire about foul play? I'll have to know anyway, and I wish you'd tell me now, before that boy comes in from fussing with the car."

Monty was filling the coffeepot. He set it on the hottest part of the stove and turned toward her commiseratingly.

"I reckon I had better tell yuh-all," he said gently. "The thing that scared me was that this man, Hawkins, come here and made his brags about how he got the best of yuh-all in that agreement. Him and Gary had some words over it, the way I got it, and they like to have had a fight—only Hawkins didn't have the nerve. He beat it out of here and Gary rode over to my place that same day and was tellin' me about it.

"I told him then to look out for Hawkins. He sounded to me like a bad man to have trouble with; or dealin's of any kind. That was three weeks ago, Miss Connolly—four weeks now, it is. I was away for three weeks, and when I got back I rode over here and found the place deserted. Gary's hawse was in the corral and the two pigs was shut up in the pen, so it looked like he ought to be around somewheres close. Only he wasn't. I hunts the place over, from one end to the other. But there wasn't no sign of him, except——"

"Except what? I want to know all that you know about it, Mr. Girard."

Monty hesitated, and when he spoke his reluctance was perfectly apparent to Patricia.

"Well, there's something else I didn't like the looks of. Up the creek here a piece, there's a grave that wasn't there the last time I was over here. I'm pretty sure about that, because I recollect I led my hawse down to the creek right about there, to water him. It's about straight down from the corral, and I'd have noticed it."

"I don't believe a word of it—that it has anything to do with Gary!" cried Patricia vehemently, and she went over and pressed her face against Gary's coat.

Monty took a step toward her but reconsidered and went on with his preparations for supper. Instinctively he felt that he would do Patricia the greatest possible service if he made her physically comfortable and refrained from intruding upon the sacred ground of her thoughts concerning Gary.

The boy who had driven the car out came in, and Monty sent him to the creek for a bucket of fresh water. The boy came back with the water and a look of concern on his face.

"I thought I heard somebody holler, up on the bluff," he said to Monty. "Do you think we'd better go see——?"

Monty shook his head at him, checking the sentence. But Patricia had turned quickly and caught him at it. She came forward anxiously.

"Certainly we ought to go and see!" she said with characteristic decision. "It's probably Mr. Marshall. He may be hurt, up there." She started for the door, but Monty took one long step and laid a detaining hand upon her arm.

"That Voice has been hollerin' off and on for five years," he told her gravely. "I've heard it myself more than once. Gary used to hear it—often. Yuh can't get an Injun past the mouth of the cañon on account of it. It was that Voice hollerin' that made Waddell sell out and quit the country."

Patricia looked at him uncomprehendingly. "What *is* it?" she demanded. "I don't understand what you mean."

"Neither can anybody else understand it—that I ever heard of," Monty retorted dryly, and gently urged her toward the one homemade chair. "Supper's about ready, Miss Connolly. I guess you're pretty hungry, after that long ride." Then he added in his convincing drawl—which this time was absolutely sincere—"I love Gary Marshall like I would my own brother, Miss Connolly. Yuh-all needn't think I'd leave a stone unturned to find him. But that Voice—it ain't anything human. It—it scares folks, but nobody has ever been able to locate it. You can't pay any attention to it. You set up here to the table and let me pour yuh-all a cup of coffee. And here's some bacon and some fresh eggs I fried for yuh-all. And that bread was warm when I bought it off the baker this morning."

Patricia's lips quivered, but she did her best to steady them. And because she appreciated Monty's kindness and his chivalrous attempts to serve her in the best way he knew, she ate as much of the supper as she could possibly swallow, and discovered that she was hungry enough to relish the fried eggs and bacon, though she was not in the habit of eating either.

The boy—Monty called him Joe—gave Patricia the creeps with his wide-eyed uneasiness; staring from one to the other and suspending mastication now and then while he listened frankly for the Voice. Patricia tried not to notice him and was grateful to Monty for his continuous stream of inconsequential talk on any subject that came into his mind, except the one subject that filled the minds of both.

The boy, Joe, helped Monty afterward with the dishes, Patricia having been commanded to rest; a command impossible for her to obey, though she sat quiet with her hands clasped tightly in her lap. Too tightly, Monty thought, whenever he looked her way.

Monty was a painstaking young man, and he had learned from long experience in the wilderness to provide for possible emergencies as well as present needs. He wiped out the dishpan, hung it on its nail and spread the dishcloth over it, and then took a small, round box from his pocket. He opened it and took out a tablet with his thumb and finger. He dropped the tablet into a jelly glass—the same which Gary had used to hold his gold dust—and added a little water. He stood watching it, shaking it gently until the tablet was dissolved.

"We-all are going to spread our bed out in the grove, Miss Connolly," he drawled easily, approaching Patricia with the glass. "I reckoned likely yuh-all would be mighty tired to-night, and maybe kinda nervous and upset. So I asked the doctor what I could bring along that would give yuh-all a night's rest without doin' any harm. He sent this out and said it would quiet your nerves so yuh-all could sleep. Don't be afraid of it—I made sure it wasn't anything harmful."

Patricia looked at him for a minute, then put out her hand for the glass and drank the contents to the last dregs.

"Thank you very much, Mr. Girard," she said simply. "I was wondering how I'd get through this night."

CHAPTER THIRTY-ONE
"GOD WOULDN'T LET ANYTHING HAPPEN TO GARY!"

Having slept well during the night—thanks to Monty's forethought in bringing a sedative—Patricia woke while the sun was just gilding the top of the butte. The cañon and the grove were still in shadow, and a mocking bird was singing in the top of the piñon beside the cabin. Patricia dressed hurriedly, and tidied the blankets in the bunk. She pulled open the door, gazing upon her possessions with none of that pleasurable thrill she had always pictured as accompanying her first fair sight of Johnnywater.

She did not believe that harm had befallen Gary. Things *couldn't* happen to Gary Marshall. Not for one moment, she told herself resolutely, had she believed it. Yet the mystery of his absence nagged at her like a gadfly.

Fifty feet or so away, partially hidden by a young juniper, Patricia could discern the white tarp that covered the bed where Monty Girard and Joe were still asleep. She stepped down off the doorsill and made her way quietly to the creek, and knelt on a stone and laved her face and hands in the cool water.

Standing again and gazing up through the fringe of tree tops at the towering, sun-washed butte, Patricia told herself that now she knew what people meant when they spoke of air like wine. She could feel the sparkle, the heady stimulation of this rare atmosphere untainted by the grime, the noise, the million conflicting vibrations created by the world of men. After her sleep she simply *could not* believe that any misfortune could have befallen her Gary, whose ring she wore on her third finger, whose kisses were the last that had touched her lips, whose face, whose voice, whose thousand endearing little ways she carried deep in her heart.

"The God that made all this *wouldn't* let anything happen to Gary!" she whispered fiercely, and drew fresh courage from the utterance.

The mottled cat appeared, coming from the bushes across the tiny stream. It halted and looked at her surprisedly and gave an inquiring meow. Patricia stooped and held out her hands, calling softly. She liked cats.

"Come, kitty, kitty—you pretty thing!"

Faith regarded her measuringly, then hopped across the creek on two stones and rubbed against Patricia's knees, purring and mewing amiably by turns. Patricia took the cat in her arms and stroked its sleek fur caressingly, and Faith radiated friendliness.

Patricia made her way through the grove, glimpsed the corral and went toward it, her big eyes taking in everything which Gary may have touched or handled. Standing by the corral, she looked out toward the creek, seeking the bushy juniper of which Monty had spoken. Carrying the cat still in her arms she started forward through the tall weeds and bushes, burrs sticking to her skirt and clinging to her silken stockings.

Abruptly Faith gave a wriggle and a jump, landed on all four feet two yards in advance of Patricia, and started off at an angle up the creek, looking back frequently and giving a sharp, insistent meow. Patricia hesitated, watching the cat curiously. She had heard often enough of dogs who led people to a certain spot when some one the dog loved was in trouble. She had never, so far as she could remember, heard of a cat doing the same thing; but Patricia owned a brain that refused to think in grooves fixed by the opinions of others.

"I can't see any reason why cats can't lead people the same as dogs," she told herself after a moment's consideration, and forthwith turned and followed Faith.

Just at first she was inclined to believe that the cat was walking at random; but later she decided that Monty Girard had been slightly inaccurate in his statement regarding the exact location of the juniper beside the creek. The mottled cat led her straight to the grave and stopped there, sniffing at the dirt and patting it daintily with her paws.

Monty was frying bacon with a great sizzling and sputtering on a hot stove when Patricia entered the cabin. Her cheeks showed more color than had been seen in them for weeks. Her eyes were clear and met Monty's inquiring look with their old, characteristic directness.

"Have a good sleep?" he asked with that excessive cheerfulness which is seldom genuine. Monty himself had not slept until dawn was breaking.

"Fine, thank you," Patricia answered more cordially than she had yet spoken to Monty. "Mr. Girard, this may not be a pleasant subject before breakfast, but it's on my mind." She paused, looking at Monty inquiringly.

"Shoot," Monty invited calmly. "My mind's plumb full of unpleasant things, and talking about them can't make it any worse, Miss Connolly."

"Well, then, I've been up to that grave. And it wasn't made by any murderer. I somehow know it wasn't. A murderer would have been in a hurry, and I should think he'd try to hide it—and he wouldn't pick the prettiest spot he could find. And I know perfectly well, Mr. Girard, that if *I* had killed a man, I wouldn't spat the dirt down over his grave and make it as nice and even as that grave is up there. And somebody picked some flowers and laid them at the head, Mr. Girard. They had wilted—and I don't suppose you noticed them.

"Besides," she finished, after an unconscious pause that seemed to sum up her reasoning and lend weight to the argument, "the cat knows all about it. She tried as hard as ever she could to tell me. I—this may sound foolish, but I can't help believing it—I think the cat was there looking on, and I'm pretty sure it was some one the cat knew and liked."

Monty poured coffee all over Patricia's plate, his hand shook so. "Gary kinda made a pal uh that cat," he blurted, before he realized what meaning Patricia must read into the sentence.

"The cat was here when Gary arrived, I suppose," Patricia retorted sharply, squaring her chin. "I can't imagine him bringing a cat with him."

A look of relief flashed into Monty's face. "That cat's been here on the place for about eight years, as close as I can figure. Steve Carson got it from a woman in Vegas when it was a kitten, and packed it out here in a nose bag hung on his burro's pack. Him and the cat wasn't ever more than three feet apart. There's been something queer about that cat, ever since Steve came up missing."

Monty started for the door, having it in his mind to call the boy to breakfast. But a look in Patricia's eyes stopped him, and he turned back and sat down opposite her at the table.

"I'd let that boy sleep—all day if he wants to," Patricia remarked. "He'll do enough talking about us and our affairs, as it is. I wish you'd tell me about this Steve Carson. I never heard of him before."

Whereupon Monty related the mysteriously gruesome story to Patricia, who listened so absorbedly that she neglected a very good breakfast. Afterward she announced that she would wash the dishes and keep breakfast warm for Joe, who appeared to be afflicted with a mild form of sleeping sickness, since Monty yelled at him three times at a distance of no more than ten feet, and elicited no response save a grunt and a hitch of the shoulders under the blankets. Monty left him alone, after that, and started off on another exhaustive search of the cañon, tactfully leaving Patricia to herself.

Patricia was grateful for the temporary solitude. Never in her life had she been so full of conflicting thoughts and emotions. Her forced resentment against Gary had suffered a complete collapse; the revulsion of feeling was overwhelming. It seemed to Patricia that her very longing for him should bring him back.

She pulled his suit case from under the bunk, touching lock and clasps and the smooth leather caressingly with her fingers. Its substantial elegance spoke intimately to her of Gary's unfailing good taste in choosing his personal belongings. The square-blocked initials, "G. E. M." (Gary Elbert Marshall, at which Patricia had often laughed teasingly), brought a lump into her throat. But Patricia boasted that she was not the weepy type of female. She would not yield now to tears.

She almost believed it was accident that raised the lid. For a moment she hesitated, not liking to pry into the little intimacies of Gary's possessions. But she saw her picture looking up from under a silk shirt still folded as it had come from the laundry, and the sight of her own pictured eyes and smiling lips gave her a reassuring sense of belonging there.

It was inevitable that she should find the "Dear Pat:" letters; unfolded, the pages stacked like a manuscript, and tucked flat on the bottom under the clothing.

Patricia caught her breath. Here, perhaps, was the key to the whole mystery. She lifted out the pages with trembling eagerness and set her lips upon the bold scribbling she knew so well. She closed the suit case hastily, pushed it out of sight beneath the bunk and hurried out of the cabin, clasping the letters passionately to her breast. She wanted to be alone, to read them slowly, gloatingly, where no human eye could look upon her face.

She went down to the creek, crossed it and climbed a short distance up the bluff, to where a huge bowlder shaded a smaller one beside it. There, with the butte staring down inscrutably upon her, she began to read.

CHAPTER THIRTY-TWO
"IT'S THE VOICE! IT AIN'T HUMAN!"

Gary had been imprisoned in the crosscut eight days, counting the time until noon. He had stretched his lunch to the third day; human endurance could not compass a longer abstinence than that, so long as the smallest crumb remained. He had drunk perhaps a quart of water from the canteen he had carried up the bluff the day before the catastrophe, and had left the canteen there, expecting to use it for drilling. With a fresh canteen filled that morning at the creek, he had something over three gallons to begin with. Wherefore the tortures of thirst had not yet assailed him, though he had from the first hour held himself rigidly to the smallest ration he thought he could endure and keep his reason.

Through all the dragging hours, fighting indomitably against despair when hope seemed but a form of madness, he had never once yielded to temptation and taken more during any one day than he had fixed as the amount that must suffice.

He had almost resigned himself to death. And then Faith, unwittingly playing providence, had roused a fighting demon within him. The wild dove had won back a little of his failing strength just when a matter of hours would have pushed him over the edge into lassitude, that lethargy which is nature's anesthetic when the end approaches, and the final coma which eases a soul across the border.

While Patricia slept exhaustedly in the cabin below, Gary babbled of many things in the crosscut. He awoke, believing he had dreamed that an automobile drove into the cañon the evening before. Nevertheless he decided that, since there was no hope of cutting away the granite wall with his knife, or of lifting the bowlder, Atlas-like, on his shoulders and heaving it out of the incline shaft, he might as well use what strength and breath he had in shouting.

"About one chance in ten thousand that anybody would hear me," he told himself. "But getting out alone is a darned sight longer shot. Trick camera work—and the best to be had—it would take, to make me even *look* like getting out. My best bet is a correct imitation of the Johnnywater Voice. But I wouldn't advise anybody to bet any money on me."

He was shouting all the while Monty was explaining to Patricia how the Voice had come to give Johnnywater Cañon so sinister a reputation. But his voice came muffled to the outer surface of the bowlder-strewn bluff, and diminished rapidly down the slope. Joe might have heard it had he been awake, since his ears were sufficiently keen to hear Gary when he shouted the night before. But Joe was asleep with his head under the tarp. And Patricia and Monty were talking inside the cabin. So Gary shouted until he could shout no more, and gave up and rested awhile.

After that he stood leaning heavily against the wall and scraped doggedly at the seams in the granite with his knife-blade.

"———and I love you, Pat. I wouldn't have you different if I could. Gary."

Patricia was obliged to wipe the tears away from her eyes before she could read the last two lines of Gary's last letter. As it was she splotched the penciled words with a great drop or two, before she hid her face in her arms folded upon a high shoulder of the rock on which she sat, and cried until no more tears would come.

After a while she heard Monty calling her name, but at first she did not care. The contents of that last letter proved that it had been written three weeks ago, evidently a day or so before Gary had ridden over to Monty's camp. She was afraid to think what might have befallen since.

It was the Voice of the rim rock that roused her finally. She stood up and listened, sure that it was Gary. To-day the beseeching note was in the Voice, and all Monty's talk of its elusiveness went for naught. It was Gary up there, she was sure of that. And she knew that he was in trouble. So she rolled his letters to her for easier carrying, cupped her palms around her mouth, shouted that she was coming, and started up the bluff.

At the cabin Monty heard her and came running down to the creek.

"That ain't Gary!" he shouted to her. "That's the Voice I was tellin' about. Yuh-all better keep down off that bluff, Miss Connolly!"

Patricia poised on a rock and looked back.

"Oh, come and help find him! That's Gary—I *know* it's Gary!" Then she turned and went on climbing recklessly over the treacherous, piled rocks.

"Come on back!" Monty shouted again peremptorily. "It's the Voice! It ain't human!"

But Patricia would not listen, would not stop. She went on climbing, bareheaded, her breath coming in gasps from the altitude and the pace she was trying to keep.

Monty looked after her, shouted again. And when he saw that nothing would stop her, he turned back, running to the cabin. There he searched frantically for a canteen, found none and filled an empty beer bottle with water, sliding it into his pocket. Then, with Patricia's sailor hat in one hand, he started after her.

When Patricia was forced to stop and get her breath, the spotted cat appeared suddenly from somewhere among the rocks. She looked up into Patricia's face and meowed wistfully.

"Oh, cat, you led me once to-day—and Gary likes you. He called you Faith. Oh, Faith, where's Gary? He *is* up on the bluff, isn't he? I believe you know! Come on, Faith—help me find Gary!"

"Meow-w?" Faith inquired in her own way and hopped upon the bowlder a few feet above Patricia. Patricia, with a hysterical little laugh, followed her.

From farther down the bluff Monty shouted, climbing with long steps. Patricia looked back, climbed another rock and stopped to call down to him.

"I'm following the cat!" she cried. "Faith is leading me to Gary!" Then she went on.

Fifty yards below her Monty swore to himself. Insanity was leading her, in Monty's opinion; he wished fervently that he had left her in town. But since she was here, and crazily climbing the bluff at the mocking behest of that phantom Voice, Monty would have to follow and look after her.

CHAPTER THIRTY-THREE
"HE'S NEARLY STARVED," SAID PATRICIA

"Damn you, Faith, where's my breakfast?" Gary stopped scraping the granite and peered balefully out at the cat, that had just hopped down mewing upon the bowlder in front of him. "I hate to crab—but I saved nearly a whole candle just on the strength of my belief in you. You might have brought me another bird, anyway. As it is, I've a darned good mind to eat *you*! You're nice and fat—I sure as heck ought to know, the way I fed you and pampered you. Come here, darn you—I could eat you raw!"

He reached out a long arm, his hand spread like a claw and made a grab at Faith. His lips were drawn back from his teeth, in a grin that may or may not have been as malevolent as it looked.

"*Gary!* Oh, *Gary!*" Patricia's voice had a sobbing gasp in it, and it sounded faint and far away.

The hand and arm hung motionless in the crevice. Gary's nostrils quivered, his eyebrows drew together. Then he reached again for the cat.

"I'm hearing things again—and this time I can't kid myself I'm asleep and dreaming. Faith, it's up to you. Either you go rustle me some grub like you did yesterday—only, for heck's sake, make it a rabbit this time—or I'll just have to eat you! A man's got to live as long as he can make one breath pull the next one after it. That's the game, Faith——"

"*Gary!* Oh, *Gary!*" Patricia's voice was closer now; at least it sounded so.

"Hello, Pat!" Gary called hoarsely, before caution warned him that it must be his fancy and no human voice.

"Gary! Where are you? Oh, *Gary!*" She was gasping for breath. Gary could hear her plainly now.

"Literally and figuratively, I'm in a hole!" he cried recklessly, mocking the intensity of his desire that the voice should be real.

"*What* hole?" Patricia's voice panted. "I lost—the cat! Where are you, Gary?"

Gary found himself clutching the rock with both hands. His knife had slid to the floor of the crosscut. His knees were weak, so weak that they kept buckling under him, letting him down so that he must pull himself up again to the opening with his hands. It was cruel, he thought, to keep thinking he heard Patricia coming to him.

"*Gary!*—Oh, Monty Girard! Gary *is* up here somewhere! I heard him! He say's he's in a hole! Oh, hurry up, why can't you?"

Gary swallowed hard. That must be Pat, he thought dizzily. Bossing Monty Girard around—it *must* be Pat!

"This way, Pat! Be careful of the slide—I'm down underground—in a hole. If Monty's coming, better wait for him. I'm afraid you'll fall. That slide's darn treacherous." Gary's eyes were blazing, his whole body was shaking as if he had a chill. But he was trying his best to hold himself steady, to be sensible and to play the game. The thought flashed into his mind of men lost on the desert, who rushed crazily toward demon-painted mirages, babbling rapturously at the false vision. If this were a trick of his tortured imagination—well, let it be so. He would meet realization when it came. But now——

He could hear Patricia panting and slipping in the loose rocks no more than a few yards away. He shouted to her, imploring her to be careful—to wait for Monty—to come to him—he did not know what it was he was saying. He caught himself babbling and stopped abruptly.

After all, it was Monty who first peered down past the bowlder and into the opening, where Gary's face showed white and staring-eyed, but with the unquenchable grin. Monty gasped the name of his Maker and turned as white as a living man may become. Then he turned; Gary saw him put up his arms. Saw two summer-shod feet with silk-clad ankles above the low shoes; saw the flicker of a skirt—and then Patricia was sitting on the bowlder where Faith had so often kept him company. Patricia cried out at sight of him and looked as if she were going to faint.

"Count of Monte Cristo—in his dungeon in the Bastille—before he did the high dive and made his get-away," Gary cackled flippantly. "Say, folks, how about a few eats?" Then his white, smiling face with the terrible, brilliant eyes, slid down and down. They heard a slithering kind of fall.

Patricia screamed and screamed again. Monty himself gave a great, man sob before he pulled himself together. He put his arm around Patricia's shoulder, patting her as he would soothe a child.

"He's just fainted," he said, his voice breaking uncertainly. "It's the shock of seeing us. Can yuh-all stay here while I beat it down to the shack and get some grub? Have yuh-all got the nerve?"

Patricia held her palms tightly to her face and fought down her panic and the horror that chilled her heart. When she looked up at Monty she was Patricia-on-the-job again; efficient, thinking clearly just what must be done.

"He's evidently nearly starved," she said, and if her voice was not calm, it was at least as steady as Monty's. "Bring a can of milk and plenty of water and a cup. And bread and a couple of eggs and a spoon," she said. "Some soft-boiled eggs, after awhile, should be all right for him. But the milk is what he should have first. Oh, if you look in my grip, you'll find a bottle of malted milk. I brought it in case the food was too bad at country hotels. That's just what I want. And hurry!"

"Yuh-all needn't be afraid I'll loaf on the job," Monty told her reproachfully; and gave her the bottle of water, and was gone before she could apologize.

Patricia crawled down to where she could look in through the opening. She could not see much of anything; just the rough wall of the crosscut where the light struck, and beyond that gloom that deepened to the darkness of night. Gary, lying directly beneath her, she could not see at all. Yet she called him again and again. Wistfully, endearingly, as women call frantically after the new-fled souls of their dearest.

She was still calling heart-brokenly upon Gary when Monty returned, puffing up the slope under a capacity load of what he thought might be needed. Slung upon his back, like a fantastic cross, was an old, rusted pick, the handle cracked and weather-checked and well-nigh useless.

"Joe's coming along behind with a shovel," Monty informed her, when he could summon sufficient breath for speaking. "Don't yuh-all take on thataway, Miss Connolly. Gary, he's plumb fainted for joy and weakness, I reckon. But he's in the shade where it's cool, and he'll come to himself in a little bit. I reckon we better have the malted milk beat up and ready to hand in. I don't reckon Gary'll feel much like waitin' for meals—when he wakes up."

Once more Patricia steadied herself by sheer will power, so that she might do calmly and efficiently the things that must be done. For an hour longer she did full penance for all her sins; sitting there on the bowlder with a cup of malted milk in her hands, waiting for Gary to regain consciousness, and fighting a terrible fear that he was dead—that they had come too late.

Joe arrived with an old shovel that was absolutely useless for their purpose. Such rocks as they could lift were quicker thrown out of the half-filled shaft with their hands, using the pick now and then to pry loose rocks that were wedged together. As for the bowlder that blocked the opening to the crosscut, they needed dynamite for that and would not have dared to use it if they had it; not with Gary prisoned in the small space behind it.

Monty worked the small rocks away from the bowlder first and studied the problem worriedly. A malapi bowlder, nearly the height of a man, fitted into the bottom of a ten-foot incline shaft with granite walls, is a matter difficult to handle without giant powder.

"Joe, yuh-all will have to beat it and get help. Three or four men with strong backs we've got to have, and block and tackle and chain—and some pinch bars. Yuh-all may have to go clear in to Vegas, I reckon—but git the help!"

Joe goggled wide-eyed at the narrow opening, stared curiously at Patricia, wiping tears from her cheeks with one hand and holding carefully the cup of malted milk in the other.

"Gosh! Kin he last that long in there?" he blurted, and was propelled several feet down the bluff by Monty's hand fixed viselike on the back of his neck.

"Uh course he'll last—a heap sight longer than yuh-all will, if yuh-all don't get a move on," Monty gritted savagely. "Fill up with water and take a lunch, and don't light this side of Vegas. Not much use stopping at the ranches this side, they ain't liable to have what we need."

He stood with his legs spread apart on two rocks and watched Joe down the bluff. Whenever Joe looked back and saw Monty standing there, his speed was accelerated appreciably. Whereat Monty grinned. When Joe disappeared into the grove, Monty turned back to the shaft, the weight of Gary's misfortune heavy upon his soul.

The first thing he saw was Patricia caressing a grimy hand and thin, bared forearm. She had just kissed it twice when she looked up and saw Monty. Patricia did not even blush.

"He drank every drop of the milk, and now he's called me a wretch and a harpy because I won't give him more," she announced triumphantly. "Do you think I'd better?"

"I reckon I better talk to him by hand," Monty grinned relievedly. "He knows mighty well he kain't bully *me*, Miss Connolly."

"I merely asked for fried chicken and gravy and mashed potatoes and asparagus with drawn butter, and ripe olives and a fruit salad with a cherry on top, and strawberry shortcake with oodles of butter under the berries and double cream poured all over," Gary explained, grinning like a cheerful death's-head through the opening. "That isn't much to ask—when a fellow's been dieting the way I have for God knows how long."

Monty blinked very fast, and his laugh was shaky. "Well, now, if yuh-all can compromise on boiled hen," he drawled, "I'll beat it back down the bluff and shoot the head off the first one I see."

"Oh, all right—all right, if it'll be any accommodation," Gary yielded, "only for heck's sake, make it snappy!"

Whereupon he forgot Monty and pulled Patricia's hand in through the opening and began to kiss it passionately.

CHAPTER THIRTY-FOUR
LET'S LEAVE THEM THERE

Love adapts itself to strange conditions when it must, and men and maids never find it less alluring. Eight days Gary had been imprisoned in the crosscut, and thought it a lifetime of misery. Yet the four days which he remained still a prisoner, but with Patricia perched upon the bowlder practically all of the time, the entombment became an adventure, something to tell about afterward as a bit of red-blooded pioneering that seldom falls to the lot of men nowadays.

It is true that Monty was there, pecking away at the bowlder with single-jack and gadget much of the time; but Patricia during those hours moved just far enough away to escape the swing of Monty's hammer, and the dialogue went on—mostly of things altogether strange to Monty Girard. Gossip of the city, plans for "The Pat Connolly" mine—in which Monty was of course included.

"I shall put three names on that location," Patricia announced, in the tone that went with the squared chin. "Whatever possessed you, Gary Marshall, to leave your name out of it—or Monty's? Do you think I'm a—a pig?"

Monty dissented to the plan, and so did Gary—but precious little good that did them. Patricia left the bowlder then, while the matter was fresh in her mind, and made the trip down to the cabin after her fountain pen so that she could have the mine as she wanted it.

"There! If the thing is worth anything—half as much as you think, Gary—two thirds of it is as much as we could ever spend and keep decently sane on the subject. And I'm sure, Gary Marshall, you'd think Monty was earning a share, if you knew how hot it is out here in the sun. The perspiration is just *rolling* off him!"

"Let up a while, old son," Gary generously implored. "I'm doing all right in here—it's a cinch, with the eats passed in to me regularly, and not a thing in the world to do. You can send out for a preacher, Monty, and I can offer my good right hand to Pat any time. Great scene, that would make! Handsome Gary entombed——"

"For pity's sake, Gary, don't j-*joke* about it!" wailed Patricia. When Monty sent a warning frown and a "sh-sh" through to the irrepressible, Gary subsided.

"Car's coming," Monty announced, glad to have the distraction for Patricia, who was crying silently with her face hidden. "If that's Joe, he's had better luck than is possible, or he's laid down on the job. I better go down and make shore. I'll bring up whatever yuh-all want to eat, when I come. If it's in the cañon," he added cautiously, remembering some of the things Gary had perversely insisted upon.

"I'm sorry, Pat," Gary murmured, when Monty's steps could no longer be heard on the rocks. "Can't you put your face right up to the opening now? Monty knocked quite a chunk of rock off a few minutes ago. And, Pat, if you knew how I wanted to kiss my girl on the lips!"

So Patricia wiped her eyes and put her face to the opening.

It happened to be the sheriff's car from Tonopah, with three other men deputized to come along and see what was taking place away over here in Johnnywater. In a little while they came puffing up the bluff to look in upon the man who had been trapped underground for considerably more than a week. They were mighty sympathetic and they were deeply concerned and anxious to do something, poor men. But they were not welcome, and it was difficult for the leading man and his lady to register gratitude for their presence.

Gary finally thought of a way out. He told the sheriff that, since there was nothing to be done at present to release him, he would suggest that they investigate the grave under the juniper. He said he thought they might be able to identify the remains of a man which he had buried there.

They took the bait and went trooping down the bluff again to do their full duty. And the last hat-crown had no more than disappeared when Patricia again leaned forward and put her face to the opening, this time without being asked.

There is nothing in the world like love, is there? When it can brighten a situation such as this and turn tragedy into romance—why, then, there's mighty little more to be said.

THE END